THE DEVIL YOU KNOW

SUZANNE CRAIG-WHYTOCK

Published by
BookLand Press Inc.
15 Allstate Parkway
Suite 600
Markham, Ontario L3R 5B4
www.booklandpress.com

Printed in Canada

Library and Archives Canada Cataloguing in Publication

Title: The devil you know / Suzanne Craig-Whytock.
Names: Craig-Whytock, Suzanne, author.
Identifiers: Canadiana (print) 20230219144 | Canadiana (ebook) 20230219152 | ISBN 9781772312157 (softcover) | ISBN 9781772312164 (EPUB)
Subjects: LCGFT: Novels.
Classification: LCC PS8605.R3467 D48 2023 | DDC C813/.6—dc23

We acknowledge the support of the Government of Canada through the Canada Book Fund and the support of the Ontario Arts Council, an agency of the Government of Ontario. We also acknowledge the support of the Canada Council for the Arts.

Dedicated to my family.
Thank you for always supporting me.

TABLE OF CONTENTS

There's a devil that sings and a devil that sighs,
A devil that laughs and a devil that cries,
A devil that's quick and a devil that's slow,
But the worst one of all is the devil you know.

I

SAMUEL

As a child, Samuel Chambers didn't know his father. He knew that he had one, of course—whenever his mother was beating him, she would scream, "You're just like your father!", the confounding words about a man he'd never met accompanying each blow. As he got older, she would often look at him with disgust and tell Samuel that he was "the spitting image" of the bastard who had left her alone with an unwanted bastard of her own.

When Samuel turned ten, a birthday card arrived in the mail. It was the only card Samuel had ever received, his mother refusing to celebrate the day that her life, according to her, was well and truly ruined. There was no return address, just the name A. Bell written in the top left-hand corner in tight, small letters. Samuel was always first out to the mailbox—his mother worked late hours and it was one of his few pleasures to sort through the bills, looking for flyers and junk mail. He would sit, neglecting his homework, using a yellow highlighter to carefully circle toys and gadgets that he knew he would never get. He would scrutinize the people in the ads, wondering if their mothers hated them too, wondering if they had friends or got Christmas presents, speculating about whether or not they felt dead inside too. With the same yellow highlighter, he would colour in the eyes of the models until they looked otherworldly and powerful.

The small envelope, addressed to S. Chambers, was tucked in among demands for payment due and the weekly grocery coupons. When Samuel saw it, he felt a thrill run through him. The envelope was powder blue and he tore it open with excitement, pulling out a card that read *Happy Birthday*! Below the greeting was a clown holding a bunch of brightly coloured balloons. Samuel hesitated, suddenly and inexplicably nervous. Why would A. Bell, whoever that was, be sending him a card? Was it a trick, like the way the boys at school would yell, "Come play with us!" but when he came, they would laugh and run away? What if there was something awful inside? He opened the card, fingers trembling slightly, and a loud, jangling version of the birthday song began to play. He shut the card quickly in surprise and fear, then slowly reopened it.

The song continued to play as he read the inscription, written in the same tight, small letters as the address on the envelope. It said, "*Congratulations on reaching this milestone, my son. I'm sorry I can't be there to celebrate with you, but I will come for you one day.*" It was signed A. Bell. Not Dad, not even Father. The formality didn't bother Samuel—he was more focused on why this person, presumably the bastard that his mother constantly referenced, would be sending him *anything*, let alone a birthday card after so many years of absolute silence. And what did it mean by 'milestone'? He quickly tore out the little tab that was creating the music—he wanted to look at it over and over, and if his mother heard...well, he'd rather not face her wrath *and* have the card torn to pieces in front of him.

The next day at school, as the recess bell rang and the other students raced for the door, Samuel held back. He approached the desk of his teacher, Ms. Ward and stood silently in front of it. She was a young woman, and kind to all of her students regardless of her personal feelings about them, but she had a special warmth for Samuel—she knew he was picked on and excluded despite her best efforts to get the other children to involve him in their games, and she saw the way his head hung down when the other boys raced by him, ignoring him.

"Is everything all right, Samuel?" she asked with concern.

He stared at the floor for a second, then looked up. She realized for the first time that his eyes were bright blue, the bluest she'd ever seen, and wondered why she'd never noticed it before. "Do...do you know what a 'milestone' is?" he asked.

"Yes...it's like an important moment in your life. For example," she continued, trying to give it some context, "when I got my teaching degree, that was a milestone for me. For other people, a milestone is graduating from high school, or a special birthday."

When she said 'birthday', Samuel's eyes lit up. "Is 10 a special birthday?" he asked.

"Maybe," Ms. Ward answered. "It depends. Why? Is it your birthday?"

"Not until tomorrow." Samuel shrugged slightly and looked out the window at the playground.

Ms. Ward took that as a cue. Inwardly, she promised herself that she would bring a treat the next day for Samuel, maybe a cupcake from the local bakery. She stood up, walked around the desk and put her hand on Samuel's back, as if to gently steer him out the door so that he could have his recess. When she touched him, he flinched and pulled away. She looked more closely and saw the discolouration of skin starting just at the collar of his t-shirt. "Samuel," she asked, "have you been hurt?"

Samuel looked down at the ground, mortified. His mother had been particularly harsh with him the night before but the thought that Ms. Ward would see it filled him with shame. He stayed silent but she insisted.

"Samuel. What happened? Show me, please."

Samuel slowly pulled the collar of his t-shirt lower, exposing the welts that tattooed his back. Ms. Ward gasped. "All right," she said, trying her best to stay calm. "I'm just going to speak to Mrs. Matulich. I'll be right back. Why don't you—why don't you feed the fish while I'm gone?"

"But it's not my turn."

Ms. Ward felt her heart about to break. "It's okay. It's your turn today. I said so. Stay here and feed the fish, Samuel."

When Ms. Ward returned, she was accompanied by the principal, Mrs. Matulich. They took him to Mrs. Matulich's office where he sat in a chair, head down, sick with fear. What would his mother do when she found out that he had shared their secret? As it was, Samuel didn't have to worry. Soon enough, a lady, a social worker from somewhere called Child Protective Services, came into the office. Samuel looked at Ms. Ward, terrified, but she knelt down next to his chair and said quietly, "You're a special boy, Samuel Chambers. Remember—you're smarter than you think and stronger than you know."

Then the lady asked him questions while Ms. Ward and Mrs. Matulich stood by. When the lady asked him who had done that to his back, he stared out the window and didn't answer. She persisted. "Was it your mother, Samuel?" He was silent for a moment, then turned and violently threw up into Mrs. Matulich's waste basket.

That was all the lady needed. The next thing Samuel knew, he was taken to an office, and after a few phone calls, the lady brought him to a house on the other side of town. It was a large house with toys in the yard and a slide and swing set. A man came out of the house. Samuel shrank back in apprehension—if his mother had taught him anything, it was that men couldn't be trusted. But the man was smiling broadly and carrying a baby.

"Hi, Lester," the lady said to the man. "This is Samuel. He needs a safe haven for a little while, and I thought of you right away. Samuel, this is Lester. He's a friend."

Samuel felt the tears welling up behind his eyes and said nothing. Lester shifted the baby to his left hip and held out his hand. "Hi Samuel. Pleased to meet you."

Samuel kept his arm at his side, head hanging. Lester withdrew his hand, cleared his throat, still smiling, and continued. "I understand you'll be staying with us for a couple of days." Maybe Lester understood that Samuel would be staying at the big house with all the toys in the yard, but Samuel certainly couldn't comprehend how that was possible. His mother would never allow it. But then Lester said, "Ms. Richardson will bring you some clothes. Is there anything else from home that you want?"

Samuel was about to shake his head when he suddenly remembered. "There's a birthday card," he whispered. "It's under my mattress."

Ms. Richardson nodded. "I'll make sure I bring it when I come back."

Samuel was lucky that he wasn't privy to the scene at his house when the social worker, along with a police officer, arrived to gather Samuel's belongings. His mother lost her mind, screaming, "You can't take him! You don't know what he is! I'm the only one who can protect him!" Her audience, although limited, was thoroughly unimpressed. She was charged with assault, Samuel was officially put into the care of the foster system, and he never saw his mother again.

Lester and his wife Veronica did their best for Samuel. What was supposed to be an initial emergency placement turned into a long-term commitment, one which Lester and Veronica were happy to take on. Samuel was no trouble—he was a timid child, not interested in playing with the other kids who came and went through the foster home, not boisterous, not a behaviour problem. They tried to engage him in 'family' activities, but he was always more content reading a book in his room than participating in game night or going on hikes with the rest of the crew. Veronica learned quickly how damaged the boy was; the first night he was in their home, she tried to tuck him into bed and he shied away from her, scrambling backwards across the mattress until he was pressed up against the wall. She knew from experience that it would take a long time to build up trust, but it was years before Samuel would allow even the slightest of touches. She considered it a personal triumph the day she put a hand on his shoulder and he looked up at her and smiled instead of twitching nervously.

He lived with them until he turned eighteen. They had, at one point, offered to adopt him, but Samuel wasn't interested. More than anything, he just wanted to be by himself, to live a quiet and ordinary life. He got a job at a local warehouse as soon as he finished high school, unloading trucks and stacking pallets. It was solitary work, and that was fine with Samuel. When he said goodbye to Lester and Veronica for good one Sunday afternoon in July, having saved up enough money to pay first and last month's rent on a bachelor apartment across town that was closer to his job, Lester shook his hand. "I'm proud of you, Sam," he said. "If there's anything you ever need…." Lester left the sentence unfinished; he had a feeling that Samuel no longer required anything from them.

Veronica, trying not to cry, put her arms around Samuel. He stiffened, and a tear escaped from her eye, knowing that even after all the years she had been like a mother to him, he was still made uncomfortable by her touch. "Will you come and visit?" she asked, pulling away and hugging herself tight to stem the flow of emotion.

"I'll try," Samuel answered. "Maybe at Christmas." But they both knew he wouldn't be back.

Samuel drifted along for years, immersed in the quiet, ordinary life he had longed for. He worked twelve hour shifts, mostly alone, avoiding the social aspects of the job: the group lunches, the Friday night bar crawls, the jokes called out from one side of the warehouse to the other, laughter echoing against the high metal ceiling. He still loved to read, loved the silence of the library, the only sound the whispery turning of pages breaking the hush. And he still looked forward to the mail, taking delight in the twist of his tiny key in the face of the mailbox door labelled Apartment 12. Other people tossed the flyers and junk mail into the recycling bin at the end of the bank of mailboxes but not Samuel. He tucked them under his arm, savouring the sensation, then pored over them at his small kitchen table, yellow highlighter in hand.

One late afternoon, he retrieved the mail as usual and his heart clenched in his chest. There was a powder blue corner sticking up from between the coupons and bills. He'd seen an envelope that colour once before. Once and never again. He still had the birthday card that had come in it, the only reminder of his childhood prior to Lester and Veronica that he ever cared to think about. Even as an adult, his bedtime ritual involved opening the now-worn and faded card, reading the words, and wondering when someone—*Father? Dad?* —would come for him. Heart hammering, he extricated the envelope and held it up to the light. It was addressed to him and again, the name A. Bell was written in the top left corner, the words printed in the familiar tight, small letters that he knew so well, having run his fingers over them almost every day of his life. He took the stairs two by two, the rest of the flyers and ads forgotten on the floor of the mailroom, clutching the envelope to his chest as if someone might try to snatch it away from him.

Back in his apartment, he stood in the kitchenette, breathing hard and staring at the envelope. Carefully, he peeled back the flap and pulled out a single piece of lined stationery. When he read what was written on it, he sank down onto the kitchen floor, weak with astonishment.

Dear Samuel, it said. *I'm sorry it's been so long since I last communicated with you. But know that I've never forgotten about you and my promise to one day come for you. I hope you can forgive me for my absence, my son. If you do, perhaps we can meet at the coffeeshop around the corner on Friday evening. I'll be there at 7 pm and I'll wait there until closing time.*

The note was signed A. Bell. Samuel shook his head in disbelief. Fifteen years was more than an absence—it was abandonment. And now this A. Bell, who couldn't be bothered to call himself 'Dad' or even 'Father', wanted to meet with him? He crumpled the note into a ball and threw it into the corner under the kitchen cupboards.

Later though, as he sat alone at the table, eating a tasteless microwave meal-for-one, he started having second thoughts. Maybe there was a really good reason why A. Bell hadn't been able to fulfill his promise for so long. Maybe he'd been overseas, or ill, or worse, in prison—Samuel's imagination ran wild. He had to know, had to understand why he'd been left with a woman who despised him. He retrieved the balled-up note from under the cupboard and smoothed it out, reading the words again carefully. There was remorse there, surely, and a desire to make amends.

On Friday after work, Samuel showered and put on his best jeans, a clean t-shirt, and a jacket emblazoned with the warehouse logo so that his father would see he wasn't some kind of bum. He wasn't even sure why he cared, but he wanted A. Bell to know that he had risen above the neglect and abuse and had made something of himself. He had butterflies in his stomach and he paced the small apartment until just before 7. Finally, it was time. He didn't know what to expect as he rounded the corner towards the coffeeshop, sweating despite the cool air. Once inside, he stood by the doorway, staring at the crowd of customers, not sure who exactly he was looking for. Would his father know *him?* Then he caught the eye of a man sitting alone at a table for two and felt a glimmer of something. The man was completely ordinary-looking, wearing khakis and a tan jacket, but Samuel was certain and, without hesitation, he went over and sat down.

The man, his father, smiled. "You came. I wasn't sure you would."

Samuel nodded. "I wasn't sure either."

The explanation, when it came, was simple and seemed sincere. A. Bell had fully intended, after sending that first birthday card so many years ago, to initiate a relationship with Samuel, but was called out of town for business without warning. It took longer than he'd planned and when he returned, Samuel and his mother were gone. "I looked for you for years," he said, his ordinary face creased with regret. "But I didn't know how to find you. Finally I was able to track down your…mother. I learned that you'd been placed in foster care, and it seemed a dead end. I was defeated for a while but then—let's just say circumstances led me to renew my search. I couldn't live with myself any longer if I wasn't able to let you know that I'd never given up hope."

Samuel's heart soared, although he didn't let it show. His father hadn't truly abandoned him; there were some holes in the story, but Samuel was willing to overlook them because the promise had been kept. It may have taken years, but his father had finally come to get him.

They talked for an hour—well, Samuel did most of the talking, surprising even himself at how garrulous he had become in his father's company. As it got close to 9 pm, his father reached out and put a hand on Samuel's arm. For the first time, Samuel didn't flinch and pull away from someone else's touch. "I have a wonderful idea," his father said. "There's a cabin a couple of hours away from here—it's been in our family for generations. Why don't I pick you up in the morning and we can go there for the weekend, really get to know each other, celebrate all those birthdays I missed? You're a Bell now, after all."

Samuel nodded, delighted. He and his father parted finally and he went back to his small apartment to pack a bag. He barely slept at all that night and was up bright and early, pacing the floor once more, only stopping to peer out the window at the street below every couple of minutes. What if it was a trick? What if, just like the boys who used to yell, "Come play with us!", his father had left the coffeeshop laughing and had disappeared again? But right on the stroke of eight o'clock, a beige car pulled up in front of Samuel's building and his father stepped out, squinting against the bright morning sun. Samuel raced down the steps to the lobby, bag in hand, then slowed as he opened the door to the street, not wanting to seem too eager.

"All ready?" his father asked, opening the trunk and stowing Samuel's bag.

Samuel nodded enthusiastically and got in the passenger side. His father opened the driver's side door and sat down behind the wheel. He turned to face Samuel and suddenly his face changed from ordinary to something else, and his eyes seemed to flash yellow. Samuel's brow furrowed and he was just about to ask what was wrong when his father pressed a piece of damp cloth into his face, with a foul odour that Samuel couldn't help but breathe in. He struggled but the ordinary man he knew as his father was stronger, relentless. As Samuel's mind started to go black, the last thing he saw was that ordinary face, so much like his own, the eyes blazing with sulphur. He felt himself falling into a half-light world of shadows and whispers, falling, falling....

From that moment on, his existence was a terrifying twilight dreamscape until the day he suddenly woke up, years later, in the driver's seat of the same beige car, head cradled in an airbag, bleeding and disoriented. And then the true nightmare began.

2

THE JIGSAW GHOST

"Finally!" I said, sitting up straighter on my stool. "Now *this* is interesting."

Gareth was by my side in two long strides, peering over my shoulder at the security camera footage we'd been studying for over 4 hours. We hadn't been able to fast forward through what had so far been a very boring kitchen scene, dimly lit by the range hood light, for fear of missing anything. About ten minutes ago, complaining that his eyes needed a change of scenery, Gareth had gone to the front of the trailer and had been staring out the window, lost in thought. Now, I could feel him behind me, scrutinizing the laptop screen to see what I was talking about.

"There," I pointed. "There's a shadow outside the doorway to the kitchen. Do you see it? It just appeared a second ago."

As we watched, the shadow grew longer. I held my breath in anticipation, not sure what was going to happen next. Then a pajama-ed figure stepped into the pool of light created by the range hood and I sighed in disappointment.

"Is that—?" Gareth pulled out the other stool and sat down.

"The daughter's boyfriend," I confirmed, as the figure, a young man in his early twenties, opened the refrigerator door and peered inside, scanning the shelves. He pulled out a glass baking pan and helped himself to a large serving of cake, presumably left over from dessert. As he stood at the kitchen island, eating his midnight snack, the family dog, a large black Lab, wandered into the room, attracted by the smell of food.

To the right of the boyfriend, laid out on the island countertop, was a jigsaw puzzle, the reason why Gareth and I, as the joint proprietors of DarkWinter Direct, were patiently studying the footage of this particular kitchen on a sunny morning in July. The email had almost been moved into our spam folder; the subject line was *Jigsaw puzzles, pieces missing,* and at first I thought it was some kind of weird ad. The DarkWinter Direct inbox was always full these days and it was often hard to differentiate between the real jobs and the junk. But when I opened this one, wondering who on earth would be trying to sell incomplete jigsaw puzzles, I realized that it wasn't an ad at all.

I know this is going to sound stupid, the email read, *but I'm convinced that a ghost is stealing pieces of my jigsaw puzzles.* And after a brief conversation with the email's author, Lisa Baxter, Gareth and I were both intrigued enough that we made the trip across the province right away. "Good to put some highway miles on the truck, too," Gareth said. The truck was new, and while the Airstream we were hauling now was considered 'vintage', it was new to us, replacing the old fifth-wheel trailer that had served as our home and office for almost three years. With the increase in business we'd seen after being involved in the capture of 'The Swamp Killer', I managed to convince Gareth that it was time to look a little more professional.

The jigsaw mystery sounded like a pretty straightforward gig. Lisa was convinced that her house was haunted by a spirit that was determined to ruin what she called her 'puzzling'. "It's so unfair!" she exclaimed, gesturing at the puzzle board at the end of the kitchen island. "Working on a jigsaw puzzle is one of the few things that I find really relaxing, but lately, every puzzle has a piece missing. And the other night, I finished a puzzle, went to bed, and when I got up in the morning, the bottom left corner piece was gone!"

Gareth and I were sure that it was probably her own forgetfulness, or that she was simply buying defective puzzles, but we were happy to try out the new surveillance equipment we'd recently acquired. "We'll hide the camera up here," I said, indicating the top of a high bank of cupboards. "It'll run for twelve hours—we can start it remotely at 8 o'clock tonight. Then we'll come back in the morning to get it and review the footage to see if it captured anything—or anyone."

She nodded fretfully, toying with a puzzle piece for a moment before popping it into the puzzle she was working on. Her shoulders relaxed and she smiled. "This is a really good one, all random-cut." Then her face creased again with anxiety. "I'll be so upset if one of the pieces goes missing and this puzzle is ruined too!"

We'd just finished installing the camera when we saw a young couple coming up the walkway towards the house. "That's my daughter Laney and her boyfriend. Please don't say anything about why you're here," Lisa cautioned us.

The couple came in the kitchen door and the girl, tall and thin, regarded us with curiosity. "Mom? Everything all right?"

Gareth gave her a strange toothy grin. "We're just here to speak to you all about the good Lord."

Laney arched one eyebrow at him but didn't respond. Turning her attention to Lisa, she said, "Sean and I are going in the back room to watch some TV. Let me know later if you want help with dinner." Then she grabbed the boyfriend's hand and led him out of the room.

I waited a moment until we could hear the television. "Okay, we're all set. Like I said, we'll turn the camera on at 8 o'clock tonight and let it run for twelve hours. If there's anything suspicious on there, we'll let you know."

"It looks like an ordinary nanny cam," Lisa said skeptically. "Are you sure you'll be able to see the ghost on it?"

"If there *is* a ghost, I'll be able to see it, don't worry." With that, we left.

Outside the house, Gareth looked at me. "Well, Verity?"

"I didn't sense anything, at least nothing wrong. The house seems perfectly normal. But you never know. I guess we'll find out in the morning."

And now, we watched as the boyfriend, Sean, finished the cake, tossing a small morsel to the patiently waiting dog. He put the plate in the sink, and I was about to tell Gareth to give his eyes a rest again, when Sean hesitated. He moved back to the puzzle and studied it, then picked up a piece, turning it back and forth between his fingers. "Do you think…?" I started to ask Gareth, but then Sean placed the piece into the puzzle, gave a triumphant fist pump, and left the room.

"I guess not," I said, answering my own question. But then something happened that made Gareth and me gasp. The dog hadn't followed Sean out of the room. He was sitting in the circle of light cast by the range hood, nose in the air, sniffing. He got up and trotted over to the island, then stood up on his back legs, muzzle snuffling across the countertop. He licked a few crumbs that Sean had left behind, then continued on to the puzzle board and ran his tongue over the pieces. Then he pushed himself back and sat down again. He seemed to be chewing something.

Gareth started laughing. "Are you kidding me?" he exclaimed. "It's the dog?"

I rolled my eyes. "Unbelievable. At least if it was a ghost, there might have been a chance of getting the pieces back."

"Well, she'll get this one back sometime later today, although she might not want it." Gareth continued laughing. The dog wandered out of the room and the kitchen was empty once more. "I need a cup of— " He stopped midsentence and leaned closer to the laptop screen, brow furrowed.

"What?" I moved closer, trying to see what Gareth was staring at.

"Right there," he answered, indicating another doorway off the kitchen that led to a small dining room. "See anything? I'm getting a shimmer."

The doorway was in shadows, but as I looked more carefully, it seemed like the shadows were taking on a form. Then the form became a woman. She stepped into the middle of the doorway and stood, arms crossed, staring up at the camera with disdain. She was older than me, maybe late twenties or early thirties, wearing a sequined red strapless dress and red high heels. She had a strand of pearls roped around her neck, and her long dark hair was swept up on one side, held in place by a rhinestone-encrusted comb.

"This case just got even more interesting," I said, after describing the woman to Gareth. He couldn't see ghosts, at least not the way I could; he was only able to detect what he called their shimmer. He explained it to me once as 'tiny sparks in a dark, empty place'. But despite not being able to see spirits, his keen sense of smell alerted him to their presence as well, sometimes long before I was aware of them. In fact, the first time we'd encountered a ghost together, he knew she was there because he said he could smell her tears...as well as the lake water her murderer had drowned her in.

I decided to edit the camera footage down to only the section where the dog was stealing the puzzle piece; if Sean wanted to eat cake at midnight, I figured that was his business. I loaded the video onto my phone to show Lisa when we returned to her house later that day. "I'd like to talk to the woman in the red dress," I said. "I wonder how we can get Lisa out of the room long enough to see if she'll manifest."

"I'm sure I can think of something," Gareth said with a twinkle in his eye, but he refused to elaborate. That was Gareth—stubborn and secretive when he wanted to be. I'd gotten used to it over the last three years, and I tolerated it, only because I knew if it was something that might put me in harm's way, he'd never keep it from me.

"Okay, *Dad*," I teased him, my small revenge for his seeming delight in excluding me from the plan. If I had a dollar for every time someone thought Gareth was my father, I'd be well on my way to being rich. Gareth hated when that happened but for me, it was worse when people thought he was my boyfriend. I generally referred to him as my business partner, but even that sounded weird. Still, that's what we were—business partners, and friends, I supposed.

"I'm nowhere near old enough to be your dad," he grumbled.

"You're the same age as my *actual* father!" I laughed. "But don't worry—you look very young for your age."

"Liar." But he smiled to himself and started packing up his duffel bag. "I'm bringing this just in case," he said, holding up the carved, rosewood box that allowed him to cross spirits over into the next plane.

"Good idea." I agreed.

We arrived back at the Baxter house mid-afternoon. When I showed the video on my phone to Lisa, she was horrified. "It was Atlas?! That little monster!" At the sound of his name, the dog sauntered into the room, looking completely innocent and wagging his tail. "How could you? That was such a great puzzle and you've ruined it! You are *banned* from this kitchen, Mister!" Atlas continued wagging his tail at his owner, oblivious to her angst.

She directed her attention away from the puzzle-eating pup and back to us. "I'll have to pack it up now. I just can't bring myself to do a puzzle when I know a piece is missing."

Gareth cleared his throat and gave me a significant look. "Well," he said, "technically, it's not missing."

Lisa was confused. "What does that mean?"

"Where does he normally, uh, do his business? The piece might be salvageable."

She grimaced. "Ew. But then again, if I used an alcohol wipe...no one else would have to know except us, right?"

Gareth smiled. "Of course not. We wouldn't tell a soul. Let me help you look—do you have any rubber gloves? And maybe tweezers...."

As they left the kitchen, Atlas following close behind them, Gareth turned and pointed to the duffel bag. "Just in case," he mouthed.

Once I heard the door to the back yard click shut, I looked around the kitchen. Nothing. "Are you ready to come out?" I called. Suddenly there was a throbbing silence, like being underwater, then a whoosh that made my ears pop.

"How did you know I was here?" a sultry voice behind me asked.

I turned quickly. The woman in the red sequined dress was standing there, arms still crossed defiantly, long hair tumbling over her bare shoulders and down her back. "I saw you on the security camera," I answered. "You were standing in the doorway over there."

"Well, it's not like I have anything better to do." She smiled and uncrossed her arms. "I see you figured out the mystery of the missing jigsaw pieces. Naughty dog."

"Who are you? Did you used to live here?"

"You can call me Samantha," she answered. "And no, I didn't live here. I was brought here a long time ago. The front of this old place used to be a doctor's office."

"So you got sick and died here?"

"Mm," she nodded. "Alcohol poisoning. New Year's Eve party. I was always the wild one. Champagne at midnight straight from the bottle one second, standing over my own dead body the next. Didn't realize I'd gotten so sauced, and the bubbly sent me over the edge. It was all a bit of a blur, but I've been here ever since."

I reached into Gareth's duffel bag and pulled out the carved rosewood box. "We can help you," I said, holding the box out towards her. The box itself wasn't particularly special; it wasn't an ancient artifact or even an antique. It was more of a symbol than anything, a conduit that joined our world with the one that Gareth and I referred to as "the world beyond the veil". Once part of a spirit's form came into contact with the empty space within the box, its energy was transported through the veil to the other side. I'd never been able to successfully use the box; Gareth was the only one who could control it, although he needed me to put a spirit into the correct mindset for the transfer to work. "My partner will be back in a minute if that's something you'd like."

Samantha laughed, a light sound like champagne glasses clinking. "No, that's fine," she said. "It's safe here. They're good people, although the mother's a bit neurotic. You've spoiled our fun though, solving the mystery. She really was hoping there was a ghost. Little does she know."

I put the box back in the bag. "If you change your mind...."

"Sure, doll," she laughed. "I'll start flicking the lights on and off. But tell me—have you always been able to see ghosts and ghouls?"

"Since as far back as I can remember," I said casually, hoisting up Gareth's duffel bag and shouldering it. "It runs in the family."

"I wouldn't like that very much. Do you ever get used to it?"

I paused. "Eventually," I said.

3

THE MILK DOOR

Gareth and Lisa had returned, he slightly disgusted and she extremely elated. The puzzle piece had, indeed, been in the dog's latest 'business' and after some digging through, Gareth was able to hold his breath long enough to extricate it from the pile of poop it was nestled in.

"It's barely damaged!" Lisa had exclaimed, already in the process of cleaning it off.

After paying us our fee plus a hefty tip, we left her with her puzzle. As we went out the door, I turned for a second and saw Samantha leaning against the doorway to the small dining room, laughing. She gave me a cheerful wave and I smiled back. When I told Gareth what had happened, what Samantha had told me, his brow creased in consternation.

"I know, I know," I responded. "But what did you want to do? Force her into the box? She's happy and she's not hurting anyone."

Gareth and I had very different ideas about our work. He firmly believed that any spirit trapped in our plane should be crossed over; it was for their own good, he insisted. On the other hand, I was convinced that just like living people, they should be able to make that decision for themselves, when they were ready, the way my sister Harmony had. I would have done anything to keep her with me, but she wanted to leave, to be with our mother and her friends on the other side. It was almost a year since that day on the beach when I'd finally let her go, and while I never regretted my decision, I still missed her terribly.

I lay there in bed later that evening, listening to Gareth's quiet breathing on the other side of the trailer, thinking about Harmony. It was always hard to do, trying to see her in my mind without also seeing John Berith, also known as The Seventh Devil, the monster who'd stolen her from me. To distract myself, my thoughts turned to Samantha and the question she had asked. Was I really used to it, to seeing ghosts and demons, spirits and malevolents, or was I just numb to it like my father had become? I'd only recently come to discover that what I'd told Samantha was true, that I wasn't the only one in my family who could see the world beyond the veil.

It was after the memorial for Harmony. Gareth had gone back to the trailer and my father had invited me to come to the house so that I could get some pictures of her and a few other pieces of memorabilia. I hadn't been back in my childhood home since the day I'd left at the age of eighteen. Harmony's room looked exactly as it had the day she'd disappeared, as if my parents had created a shrine to her. My room, of course, was being used for storage, all my possessions long gone. I sat on the edge of Harmony's bed, her favourite unicorn blanket tucked around me, while my father went through a jewelry box on her dresser.

"I thought you might like this," he said, pulling out a charm bracelet. I had given it to Harmony for her 5th birthday. He sat down next to me on the bed and sighed. I looked at him and realized he had tears in his eyes. He stared at the bracelet in his hands, fingering a tiny silver heart. "I did it all wrong. I should have told you the truth. I honestly thought I was protecting you but I was wrong."

"What are you talking about? What truth? Protecting me from what?"

"I knew about the bad houses, the ghosts, all of it. I knew the things you could see, because I've always been able to see them too. I should have told you a long time ago."

I took his hand. "Tell me now," I said. He began.

"The first time it happened to me, I was with a bunch of neighbourhood kids, and we were up to no good…

'Mikey!' a voice hissed. 'Come on, hurry up!'

'Shhhh!' I whispered back. 'Be quiet and let me listen.'

The group behind me hushed immediately. I knew they were nervous, out in the open in the driveway where anyone could see them. Could see *me*, or at least my legs sticking out of the Robertsons' milk door, the tiny cupboard where, in the old days, the milkman put the milk and other dairy products that the family ordered and then retrieved by opening a second door that led into the house. The portal was a tight fit, but I was the tiniest of the neighbourhood gang and was thereby elected to break in one bored Sunday. The Robertsons were a religious family and spent all morning and most of the afternoon at the church a few blocks away. Holy rollers, my mother called them; although I didn't know precisely what she meant, the way she said it with an air of snobbery led me to understand that the Robertsons' fervour was distasteful to her. But that fervour, and the fact that theirs was the only milk door in the neighbourhood, were exactly the things that prompted us to gather on the corner around lunchtime that day to formulate a plan.

Chicky, the oldest girl in our group at fourteen, was angry at Charmaine Robertson, for whatever reason I never knew—probably rivalry over a high school boy or some perceived favouritism at school. 'We should do something,' she proposed with malicious glee. 'Like mess up her room or write on her mirror with lipstick or…,' here she pondered thoughtfully then her eyes lit up, 'or steal that angora sweater she loves so much!'

'But we can't just break in,' Jasper Howe argued. He was only thirteen but seemed older thanks to the dress pants he always wore, no matter if we were playing soccer or simply sitting around the picnic table at the parkette.

Chicky gave us all an evil grin. 'It's not breaking in if the door is already open.'

Jasper laughed. 'Right. Like I'm sure they went off to church and left the door unlocked.'

Chicky sighed and pointed. Our eyes followed her finger. 'Brilliant,' Jasper proclaimed sarcastically, regarding the milk door. 'How are we all going to fit through there?'

'*We* can't. But Mikey can.'

And that's how I found myself half in, half out of the Robertsons' milk door on a hot Sunday afternoon in August peering around their dimly lit kitchen. I'd been recruited, with some mild objection on my part, because I was very small for nine and thin as a whip. But I was an only child, and lonely, and more importantly, I was peripheral to the gang with the hope of one day being more central to its activities, so I agreed without much pressuring from Chicky. One of the other boys hoisted me up and I crawled in on my stomach, popping the inside door with my palm and pulling myself partway through. After listening intently for a minute to make sure there was no Robertson left behind somewhere in the recesses of the old house, I called to the gang, 'All clear. I'm going in.'

I tumbled forward and onto the floor, breaking my fall with my hands. Luckily, it wasn't far down—it would have been difficult to explain to my mother how exactly I'd snapped my wrist at the parkette, which is where I'd told her I was going to be. I jumped up quickly and breathed in with jittery excitement. The air smelled of cooking oil from lunch, the dishes still on the table where they'd been left as the Robertsons rushed back to afternoon service. There was another smell beneath, more insidious, like urine and stale breath. My nose wrinkled.

'Come on, Mikey, let us in!' Chicky called through the milk door.

'Just a minute!' I whispered. I had to admit there was a part of me that didn't want the rest of the gang running around the Robertsons' house—I was enjoying the secret thrill of being in someone else's space, someone else's life. 'I'm just double checking to make sure no one's here.'

Ignoring the protestations from outside, I ventured further into the house. The living room was just off the kitchen and I went in, sat on the couch, and put my feet up on the coffee table, something I wasn't allowed to do at home. I flipped idly through a magazine, imagining myself older, all this belonging to me. Suddenly, I heard a soft cry. I leapt up, then listened, motionless.

'Connor? Connor, is that you?' The voice was frail, far away. I was about to turn around and hightail it out of there when the voice entreated, 'Connor, help me. Please, I need help.'

I was frozen, not sure what to do. But what if the person really needed help? I tiptoed upstairs to the hallway where it seemed the voice was coming from. There were several doors, presumably to the bedrooms. The doors were all shut, but there was light coming from underneath the last one on the right. As I crept closer, I could hear ragged breathing. Part of me was terrified; the other part was restless with curiosity. I reached the door and slowly turned the handle. The door swung in and I gasped in shock.

The room was harshly lit and empty, except for a small cot in the far corner. An elderly woman lay on it. She had no covers and her nightgown had ridden up, exposing her scrawny and deeply veined legs. She was shivering, although the house seemed warm enough to me. At the sound of the door opening, she struggled to prop herself up and at the sight of me, her face melted with relief. 'Connor, where have you been? I'm so cold. Please, can you get my blanket?' Her voice was a dry whisper.

There was a blue blanket lying in a heap on the floor next to the bed. I went over quickly and picked it up; it was threadbare and worn. As I got closer to the cot, I realized where the smell of urine was coming from—there was a dark stain on the thin nightgown she was wearing and more stains on the bedding beneath her. I shook the blanket out and carefully covered her, tucking it in around her legs.

'I'm so tired right now,' she said weakly as I made sure her bare feet were wrapped up. 'But maybe you can come and read to me later. Will you do that, Connor?'

'Um, s-sure,' I stuttered, not really sure at all. She sighed happily and closed her eyes. I crept out of the room quietly, but it wouldn't have mattered. She was already asleep.

When I got back to the milk door, Chicky was peering in, exasperated. 'What were you doing?!' she seethed. 'We've been *waiting*!'

I shut the milk door in her face and exited through the back door, locking it behind me to the dismay of the gang. 'Their grandma was in bed asleep. Don't worry. I snuck into Charmaine's room and wrote '*bitch*' on her mirror in lipstick.' I'd done no such thing of course, but the gang was satisfied, Chicky punching me on the shoulder in comradery before we all ran off to regroup at the picnic table in the parkette and debrief. As much as I wanted to join in the gang's gloating retelling of the adventure, voices tumbling over each with laughter and excitement, I was distracted by what I'd seen, the poor old woman alone and helpless, the thin nightgown, the soiled bedding. How could the Robertsons treat their grandmother like that?

Later, at dinner, I broached the subject with my parents. 'You know Mr. Robertson around the corner? Is his first name Connor?'

My father placed a scoop of mashed potatoes onto his plate then passed the bowl to my mother. 'I'm not sure, why?'

'Just wondering. How long has Charmaine's grandma lived with them?'

He shrugged and turned to my mother. She paused in thought, her forkful of chicken halfway to her mouth. 'Charmaine's grandma? Oh sweetie, I think her grandmother passed away a couple of years ago, but I'm pretty certain she never lived at their house. What's with the sudden interest in the Robertsons, Michael?'

I blinked hard and picked up my glass of milk, taking a swig while I scrambled to make sense of what she was saying and come up with a convincing response. The milk tasted sour – it hurt to swallow because my esophagus had suddenly closed up. Then the silence was broken by the oven timer going off, and my mother rushed into the kitchen to take out the pie she was baking for dessert. By the time she came back to the table, the conversation had been forgotten.

But I hadn't forgotten any of it. The next Sunday, I avoided Chicky and the gang, and after lunch, I made my way furtively to the Robertsons. My plan was grandiose, but I was nine and convinced that I could be a hero. I would go to the grandma's room, get her up and out of the house, and expose the Robertsons for the terrible people they obviously were, keeping her prisoner like that. I lingered behind a tree, hidden from sight, and waited until their car pulled out of the driveway. I gave it another ten minutes to make sure they hadn't forgotten anything and had to come back, then I sidled down the side of the house to the milk door. There was a garbage can by the garage and I used it to clamber up high enough to reach. I took one last look around and crawled through.

The kitchen looked the same as last time, lunch dishes littering the table, the remains of a loaf of bread going stale on the countertop alongside open jars of mayonnaise and mustard. I bypassed the living room and headed straight to the upstairs hallway. Again, the doors were all shut but this time there was no light peeking out from beneath the last doorway on the right. I made my way towards it and knocked softly as I turned the handle. The room was shrouded in darkness, the curtains on the windows pulled tight together. As I groped for the light switch, I whispered, 'It's okay. I'm here to help—' but as light flooded the room, I saw that it was empty, except for a few storage boxes. I was outraged. What had they done with her? Had she told them that I had seen her and they'd decided to get rid of her? I stormed out, flipping off the switch and slamming the door. I stood in the dim hallway fuming, my back to the room, when suddenly the air became brighter. I turned and realized that light was spilling out from under the door I had just closed.

I was frozen, breathless. My heart was pounding loudly in my ears, but over that drumming sound came another—a jagged inhalation of breath from behind the door. 'Michael,' a faint voice cried, 'is that you? I need help…'"

My father paused.

"What did you do?" I asked.

He looked at me, terror still haunting his eyes. "I ran."

I squeezed his hand. "It's okay, Dad."

"No," he said. "It's not. I ran then, and I've been running ever since. It's time to stop."

I left him that day feeling like we'd finally connected in a way that we never had before, and I vowed to keep in touch no matter where Gareth and I got to.

"We're heading out to Halifax in the morning," I said.

"I remember," he smiled, wiping tears from his eyes. "Those promises you have to keep. Are you making any progress?"

I smiled back. Uncle Pat the Poltergeist had been as feisty as always, but he really did want to cross over now that "his services" were no longer needed. As he went into the box, he exclaimed "Martha!" and his face lit up in a way I'd never seen it before. "Just a few left to go," I said to Dad. "But I'll call you when we're back in Ontario."

The last thing my father gave me before I returned to the campground where Gareth was waiting, besides the charm bracelet, was a substantial sum of money from my mother's life insurance policy. "I've been saving this for you," he said. "I know I can't make up for the past, all the lost years between us, all the missed birthdays and special occasions, but at least I can help you with your future. Your mother would want you to have it. I hope you can put it to good use."

"Well," I laughed, hugging him, "there's definitely something I have in mind. I just have to get Gareth to agree first!"

4

WEDDING BELL

It hadn't taken as much to persuade Gareth to retire the old fifth wheel trailer as I'd thought—as soon as I showed him the refurbished Airstream for sale at a really great price, he rubbed his lower back and said, "Well, it would be nice to swap that lumpy pull-out and your old mattress for proper beds."

I agreed. Lying there now, comfortable and sleepy, I turned my thoughts to the morning and the celebration tomorrow afternoon. The invitation had come while we were en route from Halifax after transitioning the souls who were still trapped on this earthly plane after perishing in the 1917 harbour explosion. During our first attempt a year ago, Gareth had been overwhelmed, but he was careful to pace himself this time, crossing over a certain number of spirits each day until they were all at peace. It had taken over a week, but in between, we got to do a little sightseeing and spend time with Mitchell Cooper, who was well on the road to recovery after our ordeal in the Greenock Swamp. The night before our last day in Halifax, we'd all had dinner together. We sat, drinking wine and eating pizza, so comfortable in each other's company as we shared our plans for the future.

"I've applied for a part-time job at the local library," Mitchell announced cheerfully. "You know how much I love books. It's only a few hours a week but it'll keep me out of trouble. And I'll still have time to do any research you need for DarkWinter Direct."

"That's wonderful—I hope you get it. They'd be fools not to hire you!" I exclaimed, flushed by the warmth of friendship and wine. "Once Gareth and I are finished with the last of the spirits tomorrow, we're heading home. Who knows what new and weird case Horace has for us? Personally, I can't wait to get back into some kind of routine." We helped him clean up and left him there, promising to contact him as soon as we knew where we were going next.

One morning, in a campsite just on the border between Quebec and Ontario, I opened the DarkWinter Direct inbox and gasped with joy. "Gareth!" I called. He was outside meditating and I hated to interrupt him but this news was too much to hold in. "Gareth, guess what?"

He opened his eyes slowly and glanced at me. "I can't even begin to guess. What's going on?"

I was just about bursting with excitement. "Horace and Quentin—they're getting married! The invitation just came—the wedding is in two weeks!"

Gareth uncrossed his long legs and stood up, stretching his lanky frame. "Well, good for them. I assume that we're each other's 'plus-one'?"

"Who else? I need to go dress shopping, and you need something a little fancier than jeans and a T-shirt, and there's the gift—what should we get them? Ooh, we can stop near Ottawa—they have a couple of great malls there, I think."

Gareth's expression was dour. "I hate shopping."

But hate it or not, he had, with minor grumbling, picked out a simply tailored suit, and it hung now in the small trailer closet next to the first strapless dress I'd ever owned. I'd never had the chance to dress up as a teenager and wouldn't have gone to my own prom even if I'd been invited. I had just started high school when my younger sister Harmony disappeared, and all the rumours and suspicions about my involvement had made me a pariah. Once in a while, someone would try to befriend me, or a boy would ask me out, but it never took long before it became obvious that it was an attempt to get juicy gossip, or worse, that the date was a dare or part of a bet. Eventually, I became a loner, ignoring the whispers and the cruel nickname "Sister Killer" that some of the other kids thought was hilarious. It was a long time ago and I'd mostly put it out of my mind, although I couldn't help hoping they felt a little ashamed when they saw all those bones being pulled out of the Greenock Swamp. The only person who had been even remotely kind to me was a boy named Eric Shah—after the media coverage of the capture of Samuel Bell, I found an email from him in the DarkWinter Direct inbox that read, "I always knew it wasn't you." I didn't respond. What was there to say—thanks?

Now, of course, despite the past, I considered myself a lucky person. I had Gareth and Mitchell, and the beginning of a new relationship with my Dad. On top of that, I had Horace and Quentin's wedding to look forward to, as well as a beautiful dress to wear.

We set out early, hoping to be at *The Echo* by lunchtime. *The Echo* was not only the name of Horace's online magazine specializing in true stories of the macabre and paranormal, but it was now the name of our new "headquarters", a sprawling old Georgian manor in the countryside that Horace had bought a few months ago. "There are too many looky-loos coming into town," he complained. The media had gotten wind of our relationship with Horace and, while the attention increased his readership exponentially, it also increased the number of people who just happened to wander by his house in Collingwood, hoping to get a glimpse of either Gareth or me.

"I have no interest in being a tourist attraction," he proclaimed, and with that, he sold the pristine turn-of-the-century Victorian home that he'd lived in for years in exchange for a house in the country that, while huge, was advertised as being in 'as-is' condition, which was to say it needed a *lot* of work. But between him and Quentin, who had moved down permanently from the North, they were well on their way to turning the derelict home into a showcase where Gareth and I had our own rooms as well as an office for DarkWinter Direct.

We pulled into the wide laneway around noon and parked in the shade under a graceful, hundred-year-old weeping willow tree that Horace declared was "the jewel of the property". It was the thing that had clinched the sale, he claimed. "I never could forgive my mother for cutting down the weeping willow that my sister Mimi and I spent so much time together under. But this one—every time I see it, I can't help but smile and think of her."

As we were unloading the Airstream, Horace came bustling out of the house. He was wearing a three-piece suit with a flour-covered apron tied over it, and he was rubbing his hands together in agitation. Quentin was following close behind and trying not to laugh.

"There you are!" Horace exclaimed. "And just in time! Gareth, I desperately need your help in the kitchen—the Yorkshire puddings simply *refuse* to rise!"

"This is what happens when you insist on doing all the cooking yourself," Quentin chimed in with a sympathetic grin. "He's been in the kitchen all morning, you know."

"Yes, and the guests will be arriving in less than three hours! Come, Gareth—I know your expertise in chemistry will come in handy with the puddings. Verity, be a dear and help Quentin with the tent people." His voice dropped to a whisper. "I've told them a dozen times where to place the stakes but they won't listen. You and Quentin will make sure it's in the right spot, won't you?"

He looked so distressed that I couldn't say no. I lay my dress carefully on the stack of luggage that we'd had taken out of the Airstream while Gareth tagged along after Horace, glancing back at me once and mouthing "*Yorkshire puddings?*"

I mouthed back, "*You'll be fine,*" then I followed Quentin dutifully to the site of the so-called tent debacle, where several workers were draping a huge canvas over the poles that spanned a section of lawn. "It looks alright to me," I told Quentin, and he laughed.

"I know. Poor Horace, god love him. He wants everything to be perfect and gets himself so worked up. I try to stay out of his way and just smile and nod. We'll stand here for a minute, then I can go in and tell him that I laid down the law. By the way, it's good to see you." He put his arm around my shoulder and squeezed. "How have you been?"

"Good. Busy. I'm so happy for you and Horace."

"Yes," Quentin beamed. "I never thought at my age I'd be getting married. It's quite an adventure."

"I can imagine that life with Horace is never boring, that's for sure," I replied.

We watched the crew erecting the tent for a while, standing together in companionable silence. Suddenly, there was a shout from behind us. We both turned to see a young man, about 25 years old, striding towards us, a huge grin on his face. "Weston!" Quentin yelled back, obviously pleased to see him. "Verity Darkwood, this is my nephew Weston Crane," he introduced us, and the young man held out his hand to me.

"Nice to meet you," he said. He took my hand and shook it firmly, then grabbed Quentin and pulled him into a bear hug. He was tall, with dark hair, and reminded me of what Quentin would have looked like at that age. They released each other after a moment, relaxed in each other's company.

"So how do you know Uncle Q.?" Weston asked, his dark eyes shining with good humour.

"Verity and her business partner Gareth Winter have been friends for a long time," Quentin responded. "Speaking of Gareth, I have the feeling he might need rescuing from Horace's puddings. I'll see you in a bit, Weston. In the meantime, I'm sure Verity can show you to the guest room—" he paused for a second, then seemed overcome with emotion. "I'm so glad you're here," he said quietly, patting his nephew's arm for a quick second, then walked off towards the house, leaving the two of us alone.

Weston cleared his throat. "So, uh...Verity—what kind of business are you in?"

The answer to that question was very complicated, so I simply said, "Oh, Gareth and I have a cleaning company—homes, offices, churches sometimes, that kind of thing. What do you do?"

"I'm a software engineer. Graduated last year, lucky enough to get a job right away. So Gareth's your business partner or your...?"

"Just my business partner," I answered, not sure what he was trying to ask. "Why don't you let me show you to your room? You can get settled and then meet him for yourself."

Weston nodded in agreement, apparently satisfied with my answer, and we headed back to the house. On the way to the front stairs, we passed the kitchen and I peeked in. Gareth was standing completely still, covered in flour, while Horace was pointing and explaining something to Quentin, his enthusiasm bordering on barely restrained mania. I stifled a laugh and Gareth looked at me, his eyes pleading to be released.

"Hang on a second," I said to Weston, then called into the kitchen. "If the puddings are no longer in danger, can I borrow Gareth back to help me get our bags up to our rooms?"

"Of course, my dear!" Horace agreed magnanimously. "He's been a wonderful help! I mean, look at these!" He tipped up a muffin tray full of golden crusted pastries. I gave him a thumbs up.

Gareth came out into the hallway, his relief obvious. "That man is a brutal taskmaster. He takes his cooking *very* seriously."

I laughed. "You have flour in your hair. Gareth, this is Weston Crane, Quentin's nephew."

Gareth started to offer his hand to Weston, realized it was coated in flour as well and thought better of it. "Good to meet you," he said.

Weston smiled. "You, too. Verity tells me that you run a cleaning business together."

Gareth hesitated, confused. I gave him a pointed look. "Ah, yes," he cleared his throat. "A cleaning business. We clean...things. Anyway, I'll go get the bags." He stalked off, slapping his thighs as he went and sending up tiny clouds of flour.

After I showed Weston to his room, I realized that it was less than two hours until the wedding ceremony was supposed to start. Gareth arrived with the bags, and we all went our separate ways to get ready. I was excited and nervous—I'd never been to a wedding, or anything remotely fancy and I was really looking forward to dressing up. The dress was a lavender satin, and I'd bought low, strappy heels that I'd practiced wearing in the trailer. The first time I'd put them on, Gareth had laughed and said I looked like a newborn foal, but it hadn't taken long to get my balance. I pulled my hair back into a sleek bun and then stepped into the dress. Immediately, I knew I had a problem. At the store, the saleswoman had zipped me up, and I hadn't even thought about what I would do if I was alone. Now, I stood there, contorting myself and willing my arms to stretch a little further so that I could grab the zipper pull. I'd just about given up when there was a knock at the door.

I opened it a crack and breathed a sigh of relief. Gareth was holding a knotted up tie—it looked like he was having as much trouble as I was.

"I haven't done this in years," he said, waving the tie and coming into the room. "I looked up some instructions, but I can't do it myself—in the mirror, everything gets reversed and I keep screwing it up." He noticed that I was clutching the strapless dress to stop it from falling off. "Fair trade," he said, tossing the tie onto the bed and gesturing at me to turn around. A few minutes later, we were both ready to go downstairs when he exclaimed, "Hang on!" and disappeared down the hall to his room. When he returned, he was carrying a small box that he presented to me with a flourish.

I raised my eyebrows questioningly and opened it. Inside was a beautiful corsage, with lavender roses and a spray of tiny white flowers. "Thank you," I whispered, removing it from the box. "How does it…?"

Gareth took it from me and slid the band over my hand to settle it onto my wrist, then he held out his arm. "Shall we?"

Outside, the scene was magical. The tent, despite Horace's misgivings, was up and fully decorated with garlands and rosettes, and a long table by the entrance held trays of champagne glasses, the bottles chilling in silver ice buckets. A small gazebo nearby was festooned with white and pink lilies, sparkling with twinkle lights, and a string quartet was playing softly off to one side. The chairs for the guests were rapidly filling and Gareth and I took reserved seats in the front row next to Weston, who was wearing a fine blue suit and striped tie. He smiled at me nervously and patted the front pocket of his blazer. "I'm the ring bearer. Have to keep checking to make sure I haven't forgotten them!"

"I'm sure you'll be fine," I reassured him. Just then, a woman, the officiant, arrived on the scene and went into the gazebo. The crowd hushed. At the stroke of four o'clock, the musicians struck up The Wedding March, and everyone's head swivelled around to see Horace and Quentin walking down the aisle arm in arm. Horace was beaming and resplendent in a white tuxedo with pink cummerbund and Quentin, who was dressed more simply in a dark suit and pink tie, couldn't have looked any happier as they approached the gazebo.

The ceremony was brief but lovely—they had written their own vows, and there wasn't a dry eye in the house when Quentin proclaimed, "I've been searching my whole life for someone like you, my wonderful Horace," his voice choked with emotion. Horace gripped Quentin's hands tightly and nodded, tears spilling down his cheeks. Then the rings were presented, Weston deftly producing them from his pocket and returning to his seat, grinning with relief. Then finally, the kiss that brought thundering applause from the guests.

After champagne toasts, there were speeches, Quentin drawing a loud round of laughter from the crowd when he quipped, "I'd say I'm looking forward to growing old with you, dear Horace, but considering we're both in our sixties, I'll have to say, 'growing *older*'!" I'd been asked to say something on behalf of Gareth and me, and despite my intense dislike of public speaking, I told the guests about the move from Collingwood and watching Horace and Quentin merge their homes, and lives, as seamlessly as if they'd always been together. Then Marcus and the rest of Horace's séance group got up and sang The Beatles' "In My Life" a cappella, causing Horace to sob into a large white handkerchief while Quentin pulled him close and kissed his head.

After the meal had been served, an incredible plating of roast beef, mashed potatoes and gravy, and Yorkshire puddings (Gareth passed his to me, stating that he "never wanted to see another one of those things" in his life, much to my amusement), additional musicians arrived and the dancing began. We watched as Horace and Quentin made their first turn around the dancefloor, then others in the crowd joined in. After a few songs, Weston turned to me and cleared his throat. "Verity, uh…would you like to dance?"

I didn't know what to say—I'd never danced with anyone before, but Gareth nudged me. "Of course she would," he answered for me, leaving me no choice but to get up and accompany Weston, who took one of my hands and put his other hand on my waist. I hesitated and looked around surreptitiously, watching what others were doing, then placed my free hand on his shoulder, as he whirled me away.

My discomfort must have been obvious and Weston tried to put me at ease by making small talk until finally, I started to relax, even laugh a little. But then he caught me completely off-guard. "So," he began, "Uncle Q. spilled the beans about your 'cleaning business'."

"Weston, I— " I wasn't sure how to respond.

"Call me Wes, please—everyone does. And it's okay. I may have done a degree in Computer Science but that doesn't mean I don't believe in—well, you know. I think it's cool, and if you ever need any help, I'm pretty good at researching and getting information that might otherwise be hard to find. I've been helping Uncle Q. for years with his *Mysterious Events and Unsolved Crimes* website, and I'll be doing a lot more of that on the side, especially now that he has his hands full with the honeymoon and the renovations and everything else." He paused, his eyes sparkling mischievously. "And I'd love to get to know you a little better."

I could feel my face getting warm. "Well, Wes, that's—kind of you to offer. I'm sure Gareth and I would appreciate the help, if needed." The song ended and we went back to the table, my head spinning with both the champagne and what Wes had said. When the guests all began making their way to the head table to get pictures of Horace and Quentin cutting the cake, I begged off, making the excuse to Gareth and Wes that my feet were sore from the new shoes.

I was sitting alone, enjoying the sight of Horace and Quentin passing out plates of cake when something outside the door of the tent caught my attention. I turned casually to look—a figure was standing there in the dark, watching. A guest, no doubt, getting some fresh air. But suddenly, there was a flash of yellow as a pair of otherworldly eyes bore into mine. I leapt out of the chair, knocking it over, and my hand flew to my mouth to stifle a scream as the figure, a man wearing khaki pants and a tan jacket, an ordinary man in every way except for those eyes, stepped into the light and began walking towards me.

5

CRIES IN THE NIGHT

Gareth was by my side like a shot, his long legs covering the distance in a matter of seconds. "What's wrong?"

I turned to him, distracted by his appearance, then pointed to the doorway, my hand shaking. The figure was gone. "I…someone was there," I stammered.

"Who?"

"Samuel Bell," I whispered. *"John Berith was…in him."*

Gareth's eyes went wide. "No. That's impossible." He pulled out his cellphone, turning on the flashlight and stormed out of the tent. I waited, pacing. He was back after a few minutes, brow furrowed. "There's nothing out there that I could see. And I don't sense anything."

"Well, it was Samuel Bell. I saw him with my own eyes! And *his* eyes were yellow!" I was on the verge of tears. Everyone else was still at the front, taking pictures and eating cake. Weston looked back at us, curious, and I gave him a fake smile, hoping he couldn't tell that I was trembling with fear.

"Verity, come on. Think about it," Gareth said softly. "Think about what you're saying. John Berith is gone and Samuel Bell, who's been comatose for months in the secure ward of a penitentiary hospital hundreds of miles away, suddenly appears at Horace and Quentin's wedding? How did he get here? And where did he go?"

"I—," I crossed my arms across my chest and stared out the door. "I don't know. But I was sure I saw him...."

"Look, it's been a long day. A long year, for that matter. You're tired, you've been drinking champagne, and it's late. Maybe the light was playing tricks with your eyes or—," he hesitated. "Maybe you imagined it?"

I sighed, embarrassed. "Maybe. I don't sense anything either. But I was so sure."

"You know if Bell had escaped, we'd be the first people they'd contact. But in the morning, we can do some research, see if there are any reports, any indication that he's not *exactly* where he should be."

I nodded in acquiescence, suddenly exhausted. "I think I'll go up to the house, try to get some rest. Say goodnight to Weston for me, will you?"

Gareth offered to walk me back, but I turned him down. He was right—John Berith, The Seventh Devil, was gone, Samuel Bell was incapable of just appearing out of thin air, and there was no glimmer, no angry tendrils reaching out for me. But still, for the first time in months, it took me ages to get to sleep, and when I finally dozed off, I was plagued by vague nightmares about a man with yellow eyes.

Finally, around 4 am, I gave up and started searching news sites on my phone for any information to prove that I could have been right, but there was nothing. A little after 6, I could hear the house stirring, so I went down to the kitchen. Horace was busy, happily bustling around and getting breakfast ready, the consummate host despite the fact that he must have been as tired as I was.

"Verity, my love!" he exclaimed. "You missed the pinata at midnight, but dear Gareth said you were feeling unwell. I trust a good night's sleep has restored you!"

I sat down at the kitchen table and gave him a small smile. "I'm all right, just road weary. I feel better this morning." It was a lie, but I didn't want to spoil Horace's good humour.

"Oh, I'm so glad to hear it!" he exclaimed. "Because a new case just came in. A very *intriguing* situation involving—well, I won't say anymore until Gareth arrives. I want to see the look on your faces when you find out who...oh, I really mustn't say anything else!" He gave his own hand a light slap and laughed. "Here you are, my dear." He passed me a plate heaped high with scrambled eggs, toast, and bacon. "Just what the doctor ordered!"

I accepted the plate gratefully and dug in. By the time I was finished, Gareth had made his way downstairs as well. "Oh good, you're here!" Horace put another breakfast plate in front of Gareth enthusiastically. "I was just talking to Verity about—but oh, maybe I should wait until you've had a chance to eat," he continued coyly.

Gareth raised one eyebrow. "Talking to Verity about what?"

"Horace has a new case for us," I said, "and he's dying to tell us about it."

"I *am*. And now that you're both here—well, you've heard of Milana Cordero?" Horace looked at us both intently.

"The singer from Vancouver? Isn't she the one who married her producer?"

I was surprised—I didn't think Gareth knew anything about popular culture. "Yes, her much younger producer," I added. "What about her?"

Horace's voice became sober. "Not many people know this, but she and her husband suffered a terrible loss not too long ago. A child. Stillborn at 6 months. It wasn't covered by any of the news outlets—they wanted to keep it quiet because...."

We waited. Finally, Gareth sighed. "Because why, Horace?"

"Because she's being haunted by the ghost of the child. Or at least so her husband Gabriel informs me. She's just about at her breaking point, according to our communication. She hears it crying in the night and it's tearing her apart. He's desperate for someone to help her. What do you think?"

"Vancouver?" I was hesitant. "Oh, Horace, I don't know. It's been a long couple of months—I just don't have the energy to go all the way out to the West Coast."

"Well then, you needn't worry, my dear!" Horace was elated. "Milana and her husband live in Toronto now. And as for not having any energy, you don't need much. They live right downtown. You could take the train in, be there and back in a day or two. The fee they're willing to pay will more than cover all of that, as well as hotel rooms if you decide you'd rather stay over and do a little sightseeing. Or shopping!" Horace looked back and forth between Gareth and me expectantly.

Gareth was quiet for a minute, processing. I knew he understood my reasons for wanting to stick around home base for a while, but after a minute he said, "I think that'll work. And shopping? Well, you know how much we both like to shop."

Horace clapped his hands together. "I'll email them right away, let them know to expect you. I'll drive you to the train station once you're finished packing up."

He bustled out of the room, and I gave Gareth a pointed look. "Really? We *both* love shopping? Who do you think you're kidding?"

"Two things," Gareth said. "First, we could use the money. Second, you could use the distraction. I can tell that you're still upset about last night—this might take your mind off it. We can go, check out the ghost—" he stopped abruptly as Wes came into the kitchen. "—the mess," he continued, "and see how bad things really are."

Wes laughed. "Don't worry about me. I told Verity last night that Uncle Q. had filled me in on your 'cleaning business'. Anything I can do to help?"

Gareth shook his head and stood up to put his dishes in the sink. But I had a sudden idea—I knew Gareth wouldn't like it, but I had to ask.

"Wes, you told me last night that you were good with computers and could do research for us if needed. Is there any chance you could find out the status of a patient up at Strongpoint?"

"Isn't that the secure psychiatric prison? I probably could. What patient are you interested in?"

Gareth gave me a warning glance but I ignored him. "His name is Samuel Bell. I was just wondering if he was still incarcerated."

"Samuel Bell?" Wes's eyes widened. "The Swamp Killer? You and Gareth helped put him away for life—why would he have ever been freed?"

Gareth interjected. "No one's saying he *has* been. Just check it out, all right?"

Wes piled his plate high with bacon and eggs. "I'll get right on it, as soon as I have breakfast."

I got up and put my plate in the sink too. "Gareth and I are heading out for a while. Here's our contact number if you find out anything."

I gave him one of our business cards and he tucked it into his pocket with a grin. "I'll keep you posted. Shouldn't take too long to get the answer."

Suddenly there was a flurry of joyful honking from out front. We all turned in the direction of the music, startled. "Is that—?" I started to say, and Gareth finished for me.

"Yes, it sounds like a riff from *Snowbird*, that Anne Murray song."

Wes laughed. "Looks like Uncle H. is taking his old Tin Lizzy out for a spin."

"I think that's our ride," I said to Gareth. "Better get packed!"

When we came out the front door with our bags, Horace was sitting in the driver's seat of his prized vintage

1966 Austin Healey 3000 convertible. "Gorgeous day to go topless, don't you think?" he yelled to us. "Ooh, that was cheeky of me! Are you ready? I already got a response from Gabriel. He's relieved you're coming, and more than happy to cover all costs, so I've booked you into the Ritz-Carlton for tonight. You'll be at Union Station by noon if we leave now. Hopefully, things will go smoothly and you'll have some leisure time."

The car was cherry red with a black leather interior, and it was Horace's pride and joy. He rarely drove it, and only if there wasn't even a slight hint of rain. Gareth stood there holding our overnight bags, a skeptical look on his face. "How many people does this thing seat?"

Horace chuckled. "Two up front, and two in the jump seats. One of you can sit back there with the bags—Gareth, I'm sure you won't mind, will you? We don't want Verity getting too windblown. Oh, and don't worry, I've had seatbelts retrofitted for safety!"

Gareth gave a resigned sigh and squeezed into one of the small jump seats, his long legs practically up around his chin and his arm resting on our overnight bags. I settled into the luxuriously comfortable front seat, feeling slightly guilty, but not guilty enough to want to swap places with him.

"Today must be a special occasion," I remarked, as Horace put the car into gear and we took off.

"Indeed it is, my dear," he answered, downshifting and accelerating. "I'm married!!"

Horace's elation was contagious, and I soon found myself enjoying the freedom of driving with the top down. The previous night seemed like a bad dream in the bright light of day, and I decided to put it out of my mind. If there was something to it, which I doubted, Weston would let us know. Until then, I needed to focus on the task at hand, which Horace had somberly announced he was calling *'Cries In The Night'* for his feature in *The Echo*.

Gareth and I boarded the train and took our seats, Horace waving to us as we pulled away. It wasn't long before we were at Union Station, trying to make our way through the throngs of travellers coming and going in the busy concourse. Gareth found a station map that led us to the exit, and we found ourselves on Front Street. "Just a couple of blocks that way," he pointed, and we set off towards our hotel to get changed and freshened up before meeting the Corderos.

"Aren't you even a little excited?" I teased Gareth on the elevator after we'd checked in. "She's won a lot of awards, hasn't she?"

"Three Junos and a Grammy," he answered immediately. "But whatever's haunting her doesn't care. The dead don't discriminate."

It was obvious that Gareth was downplaying his enthusiasm, and I couldn't help smiling to myself when I heard him singing what sounded like a Milana Cordero song through the wall of our adjoining rooms.

When we knocked on the door of their Bay Street penthouse, I could tell that Gareth was holding back nervous energy by the way his lips were pressed tight together. And he'd neatly combed his steel-gray hair instead of just running his fingers through it the way he normally did. Gabriel Cordero answered the door and when he saw us, his relief was tangible. "Come in, please," he said quietly in a heavily accented voice. "Milana is in the living room."

He ushered us through into a large open area with floor to ceiling windows. The view was breathtaking and I was so distracted that, for a moment, I didn't see the woman curled up in the corner of a huge white sectional sofa. It wasn't until Gabriel said, "They're here," and she stirred that I realized she was in the room. The view was nothing compared to her. Milana Cordero had to be one of the most beautiful women I'd ever seen, despite the dark circles under her red-rimmed eyes. She looked up at us;

it was clear that she'd been recently crying, and my heart went out to her immediately. I stared at her and the room was silent until Gareth put his duffel bag down gently onto the carpet and cleared his throat, spurring Gabriel to move closer to his wife. He sat down next to her and held her hand, looking up at us expectantly.

I took the initiative. "Ms. Cordero, I'm Verity Darkwood and this is my business partner Gareth Winter. You know why we're here, so tell us what's going on. Start at the beginning."

Milana began to speak but then stopped, dissolving into fresh sobs. Her husband's expression was pained. "A few weeks ago, Milana and I...we lost a baby. Our first. A little girl, stillborn—" his voice caught for a second and he paused. "Stillborn at 6 months."

"I'm so sorry," I said.

"No one knew, except our families. We kept it out of the papers, stayed close to home, telling people that Milana was working hard on a new album. The paparazzi can be so thoughtless, so cruel."

Gareth nodded in sympathy. He and I had certainly had our share of that in the aftermath of Samuel Bell's capture, Gareth particularly, once they got wind of his 4 year-old sister Julia's death. One reporter had been especially relentless, calling at all hours and even going as far as to suggest Gareth might have had something to do with her drowning, even though he'd been a child himself at the time.

"We only agreed to this...meeting because Horace promised us absolute anonymity," Gabriel continued. "But we had to do something. It's taking such a toll on Milana."

"And what exactly is 'it'?" I prompted.

Milana pressed the heels of her palms hard into her eyes, then took a deep breath. "I hear the baby crying. All the time. I know it's impossible; I mean, she died before she ever got to make a sound, but I hear her all the same. She's crying, and I can't help her. It's torture!" With that, Milana started weeping and Gabriel put his arm around her, looking at us pleadingly.

"She's exhausted. Can you just take a look around, and if you find anything, can you…do something about it? Horace said you were very good."

Gareth stood and picked his duffel bag up, slinging it over one shoulder. "Of course. Is the crying specific to any room, or do you hear it everywhere?"

Milana sniffed. "The nursery," she whispered, pointing down a long hallway. "Second door on the right." She buried her face into Gabriel's shoulder as we left the living room.

The door to the nursery was closed. "Thoughts?" Gareth asked before we went in.

"I don't know," I answered. "I'm sensing *something*, but it doesn't feel like a spirit."

"Malevolent?"

"No, I'm not sensing dark energy either. It's different, but familiar at the same time. Are you ready?"

Gareth nodded. I opened the door, walked in and immediately shuddered. The nursery was beautifully decorated with care and love, that was obvious, from the pastel bunny mobile over the white crib to the rocking chair in the corner. But everything in the room was splashed with what looked like black tar; the plush white carpet was soiled, and the wallpaper, with its motif of happy pink, blue, and green animals was dripping with black. "Ugh. This reminds me of that church in St. Cecile," I said.

Gareth's brow furrowed. "Why?"

I gestured widely at the walls and floor. "All of this, although the smell isn't the same, thank goodness." Gareth scanned the room, still perplexed. "Wait, can't you see it?" He shook his head and I described to him what I saw.

"I don't see any shimmers, and you don't sense the baby, so what is it?" he wondered.

Suddenly, there was loud crying from behind the rocking chair. "Did you hear that?" I whispered.

Gareth nodded. "I actually did. Interesting." He knelt down to open the duffel bag. I walked slowly towards the rocker, which was moving back and forth slightly, apprehensive and worried. What if it *was* the baby behind there? The thought of its spirit, tiny and alone, was heartbreaking. But when I peeked around the chair, what I saw made me take a step backwards in shock.

"What is it?" Gareth had the box in his hand, ready, but I waved him off.

"I—I'm not sure," I said quietly. "It's a small orb covered in what looks like tar, about the size of a bowling ball." I peered around the rocking chair again, and the cries lessened in intensity. "It's not a spirit, and I'm not sensing anything malevolent about it either. You can try the box, but I don't think it will work."

Gareth approached, the carved rosewood box in one hand. He opened the lid with his other hand and crouched down by the side of the chair opposite me. The little ball didn't move, but its cries turned to whimpers. It didn't seem to be capable of harm, so I reached out towards it and it fell silent. I touched it tentatively. When my fingers made the connection, I was flooded with a sensation that I knew all too well, and then I understood exactly what the orb was. I stood up, my eyes filling with tears as waves of dark despair washed over me.

"What's the matter?" Gareth asked, concerned. He put the box down and started to reach into the bag.

"No," I stopped him. I wrapped my arms around myself tightly and took a deep breath. "Nothing in the bag is going to help Milana. This—this is grief, pure and simple. She's somehow made it tangible. It's like a physical extension of her misery."

"So how do we…transition it?"

"I don't think we can." I went to the door, and as I did, the crying began again, increasing in volume the further away I got. I turned and walked back towards the rocking chair, and the cries transformed into soft whimpers again. I sat down in the chair and began to rock. The room was silent. Gareth and I stared at each other, the revelation hitting us at the same time.

Back in the living room, Gabriel was still soothing Milana, stroking her long dark hair and whispering to her. When he saw us, he stood up expectantly. "Gareth will fill you in," I said. "I need to speak to Milana alone." He nodded and gestured for Gareth to follow him into the kitchen. I sat down on the sectional across from the singer. "Milana, when was the last time you were in the nursery?" I asked gently.

She raised her face to mine. Even in her suffering, she was stunning. "You look very young," she answered, not addressing my question. "I don't suppose you have any children."

"No. Not yet, anyway."

"When you find out you're expecting, finally, after so many years of trying, it doesn't take long before you're not just having a baby anymore. You begin imagining the first step, the first day of school, the day she graduates from university, maybe even from medical school like her grandfather. Maybe the two of you perform a duet together and everyone says how alike you are. You imagine the children *she'll* have, the family Christmases—" she stopped, her voice choked with emotion. "To answer your question, I haven't been in that room since the day I came home from the hospital. I can't. I just can't go in there. It's like losing the rest of my life all over again. I hope to god you never experience that."

I didn't tell her that I already had, how the loss of Harmony was the same to me. But I knew what the solution was.

"You have to open the door and go in. It's not the baby waiting for you in there. She's already gone on; she's at peace. But you're not, and what you've done is given your grief a form and a voice. And the more you leave it alone, the larger and louder it will get. You need to be with it, and eventually, you'll both find comfort."

She stared at me. "I *can't*," she whispered.

"You can," Gabriel said from across the room. "We both can. Together." He came over and took her hand, lifting her up. "Thank you," he said to Gareth and me. We watched as they walked down the hall together and stood facing the door. Milana's shoulders heaved with sobs as she turned the handle on the door and then they both disappeared inside.

6

MORT STERVEN

Gareth and I waited in the living room for about an hour. The door to the nursery finally opened, and Gabriel came out. Before he shut the door again, I was sure I could hear soft singing. Gabriel's face was still wet with tears, but he looked like an overwhelming burden had been lifted from him.

"She says everything is much more quiet now. It's not completely over yet, but at least we know what this is, and how to...manage it. I've just come to get her notebook—she says she has an idea for a new song and wants to write it down right away. She's calling it "I Loved You Before I Knew Your Name". I can't thank you enough for your help—and your kindness. Losing a child is a terrible thing."

"I know," Gareth and I both said in unison.

Gabriel gave us a perceptive look. "I believe you both do."

He returned to the nursery with a notebook and pen. We let ourselves out and went back to the hotel.

I was emotionally drained from our experience with the Corderos, so much so that after dinner in the hotel restaurant, when Gareth suggested taking some time to visit the Art Gallery, I had to beg off.

"Come on," he implored, sitting on the sofa in my hotel room. "They're showing a special night exhibit this month called 'Heaven and Hell'. Fascinating stuff."

"As much fun as that sounds, I think I'll just stay here and work on our report for Horace. You go on—find out *all* about the afterlife for us," I said ironically.

"All right, I'll go on my own. But I hope the subway isn't too busy. 'Hell is other people', as Sartre once wrote, and a crowded subway car is proof of that." He left, promising to bring me back a souvenir.

I pulled my laptop out of my bag and sat cross-legged in front of it on the bed, trying to decide what to write. I'd never seen anything like that black orb before—I didn't even know it was possible that grief could become corporeal. And if it could, why wasn't I haunted by my *own* grief? Maybe because I'd kept running from it for so many years, and then when I stopped running, I found Harmony again. Who knows what might have happened if I hadn't been able to hold her hand one last time? Would I be sitting here now with only a ball of misery huddling in the corner to keep me company? I shook off the thought and tried to write, but I was exhausted. It wasn't long before my eyelids grew heavy, and I curled up on the bed next to the laptop.

Suddenly, I was standing in the middle of a quiet residential street facing an ordinary-looking house. As I watched, the house itself seemed to take a deep, angry breath, and I recognized with a shudder that it was one of the bad houses. I'd always known as a child whether a house was good, a place where children were happy and parents rarely fought, or whether it was bad, with dark secrets and bruises—or worse. I could have walked down any street in the country and reflexively told you in which house a murder had happened just by looking at the front door. And while the house I was currently observing in my dream wasn't a death house, I certainly didn't want to go in. The side door opened and a young boy, around ten years old, came out. He was carrying a soccer ball, which he dropped and started kicking listlessly against the wall of the house. Then, with a start, he noticed me. Tucking the soccer ball under his arm, he walked to the end of the driveway and spoke.

"Who are you?" he asked. "Why are you staring at my house?" He was thin, with ash-blond hair and dark circles under his blue eyes. The arm wrapped around the soccer ball had a faint bruise on it, and I realized with dread that it was in the shape of human fingers.

"I'm Verity," I said. "What's your name?"

"Verity?" He took a step back, wonder in his eyes. "She told me about you."

"Who told you about me?" I asked, but just then the side door opened again, and a woman came rushing out.

"Thomas!" she hollered. "How many times do I have to tell you not to talk to strangers?!" With that, she grabbed him by the arm. He dropped the soccer ball and it bounced down the driveway towards me as she hauled him roughly into the house. Right before he disappeared, he looked back, terrified.

I was stunned. Who was the boy? Was he real, or was this just my imagination again? I felt like I might be losing my mind and I started to turn away when something touched my foot. It was the soccer ball, but now, instead of familiar black and white hexagons, it was painted with red, white, and blue stripes. I felt a scream rising in my throat and then I heard a low, awful laugh coming from behind me. I spun around and *he* was standing there, as ordinary as ever except for the yellow that flashed in his eyes.

"This one is mine," he snarled, "and if you get in my way, your precious sister will be lost forever!"

I picked up the striped ball and heaved it at him, but he put his hand up and the ball exploded, pieces flying everywhere. One of them hit my leg and as I looked down, it transformed into Harmony's origami unicorn. His laughter filled my ears and the scream that had been building in my throat finally broke through, wrenching me apart, then someone was shaking me hard, calling out my name, and the street faded away into black.

"Verity, wake up!" Gareth was there in my room, his hand gripping my arm, trying to pull me out of the nightmare. I slowly opened my eyes, flooded with relief when I saw the familiar hotel room and Gareth sitting on the edge of the bed, his face full of concern. "What's going on? I messaged you when I got back but you didn't answer so I assumed you were asleep. Were you having a nightmare? I could hear you screaming through the wall."

I struggled to sit up, my head still spinning. "I—it was so real. There was a boy. 'Thomas', the woman called him. And then Berith was there, threatening me, that if I didn't leave the boy alone, he would—well, I'm not sure what he meant but it had something to do with hurting Harmony. How is any of this possible? Am I going crazy?"

Gareth slowly shook his head. "I don't think so. In fact, combined with what happened at the wedding, this is raising a lot of red flags."

"But Samuel Bell has been comatose for almost a year. Why is this happening all of a sudden? I wish Wes would call, settle the matter once and for all."

"But don't you think if Bell *had* escaped, we'd be the first people the authorities would contact? Surely we'd have heard about it by now." Gareth considered things for a moment, then said, "Regardless, I think we should get in touch with Mitchell. You and he have always had that connection—maybe he's been having dreams or visions as well."

I grabbed my cellphone and dialed Mitchell Cooper's number. It rang and rang until the answering machine kicked in, so I left a voicemail asking him to call me as soon as he could. "Halifax is an hour ahead of us—maybe he's gone to bed," I wondered. Mitchell was only in his early sixties, but our involvement with Berith had taken its toll on him physically and mentally. We'd been hoping to see him at the wedding, but he had messaged two days before that he didn't think he'd be able to make the trip. I tried not to worry, but he was by himself out there—at least Gareth and I had each other for support, as well as Horace and Quentin.

"I really wish I could convince Mitchell to move here closer to us," I said to Gareth.

"Well, when he calls back, ask him again. I'm sure Horace could use him at *The Echo*," Gareth suggested. "At any rate, I got you a little gift from the Art Gallery. I'll be right back."

He went through the adjoining door and when he returned from his room, he handed me a postcard. "This painting is called *Satan Comes To The Gates Of Hell* by William Blake. Although, considering the circumstances, maybe this isn't something you want to see right now."

I examined the postcard, reading out loud the description on the back, "'This scene depicts Satan confronting Sin and Death at the Gates of Hell'. Huh. Interesting." I put it on the night table face down. "I'll take a closer look tomorrow—in daylight." I laughed lightly but Gareth could tell I was still shaken by the nightmare.

"Do you want me to stay here tonight?" he offered. "I can sleep on the pull-out couch."

"No," I sighed. "I'll be okay. I'll find a good comedy to watch on TV, and hopefully get some sleep without any demonic visitors."

"I'll leave the adjoining door open and if you need me, just knock," Gareth said, then he left for his own room. I did as I told him, finishing up my report for Horace, then watching a few episodes of an old sitcom until my eyes got heavy again. This time though, my sleep was seemingly dreamless and I woke up the next morning feeling more calm, if not really refreshed. After a quick breakfast, we walked back to the train station and boarded our train.

The car attendant directed us to our seats, a foursome at the back of the car. When we got there, a man was already occupying one of the window seats. Only the top of his head was visible—the rest was hidden behind the newspaper he was engrossed in. He didn't even glance at Gareth and me as we took seats opposite him. I stared at my cellphone, perturbed, then placed it on the narrow table between us. "I don't know why Mitchell hasn't called back yet," I said quietly to Gareth. "It's not like him."

"Don't worry," Gareth reassured me. "You'll hear something soon."

The train filled up with passengers and then we pulled out of the station. The four-seater across the aisle from us was taken up by two boys around the age of fifteen and their backpacks. They were torpedoing a hacky sack back and forth at each other as hard as they could and laughing riotously. Gareth frowned and pressed his lips tight together, obviously annoyed. Then the car attendant came through the doors with the snack cart.

"Can I get you anything?" he asked. "Coffee, tea, snacks?" He had a slight speech impediment. I shook my head and Gareth ordered a coffee but the man opposite us didn't respond; he kept reading his newspaper. I leaned forward slightly, trying to see what was so interesting, but as I did, the pictures and text seemed to change and rearrange themselves on the page. I closed my eyes tight for a second then reopened them—there had been a large photograph of a bridge on the front page, but now there was a picture of a building on fire. I was about to say something to Gareth when there was a commotion across the aisle.

"Smartasses," the car attendant said under his breath as he wheeled the cart away. The two boys were giggling and making fun of his lisp. The man sitting across from me sighed and lowered his newspaper, neatly folding it and placing it carefully on the table between us. I was surprised to see that he was wearing mirrored sunglasses, and for a second, I could have sworn I saw an elderly woman reflected in them. He turned his head towards the two boys and spoke.

"James Thornton," he said, in a voice that was rich and deep. One of the boys stopped laughing and turned to face the man, the mocking grin dropping from his face. "You're a better person than that. Remember to treat people with respect and you just might be destined for great things."

The boy seemed entranced. "You're right," he answered wonderingly. "I *am* better than that." Then he directed his attention to his friend and said, "Stop making fun of everyone. It's childish and rude."

"Screw you, Jimmy," the other boy retorted huffily, giving us all a dirty look and crossing his arms in embarrassment. They both fell silent.

Gareth looked at the man. "Impressive," he said. "Thanks. Now I can enjoy the ride in peace."

"It's my pleasure, Gareth," the man smiled, his eyes hidden behind those mirrors. I examined him more closely. He was wearing a beautifully tailored cashmere suit, and as he reached for the newspaper again, I couldn't help but notice a very expensive-looking wristwatch on his arm.

"Hang on," I said, as he was starting to unfold the strange newspaper. I gestured at Gareth. "How did you know his name?"

The man chuckled. The sound was young and light, and as old as time all at once. "I must have heard you call him that, Verity."

I sat back in my seat, annoyed and bewildered. "And how do you know *my* name? Or that boy's?" I demanded. Gareth began to rise threateningly, but I put my hand on his arm. "Wait," I said, then I turned my attention back to the man, who was regarding both of us with a certain amount of amusement. "Who exactly are you, and what do you want?"

The man smiled broadly. "Oh, don't worry," he said. "I'm not here for either of you. At least not yet. But we do have a…mutual acquaintance in common, an acquaintance who has been giving both of us a lot of trouble lately. And you can call me Mort. Mort Sterven."

Gareth glowered at Mort Sterven. "What 'acquaintance' would that be?"

"Does the name 'John Berith' ring a…Bell? Oh," he snickered. "Pardon the dreadful pun. It's been so long since I've had an actual conversation with someone that didn't involve them crying and begging." He examined his nails and then picked an imaginary piece of lint off his lapel.

"John Berith is gone," Gareth said softly but forcefully. I nodded in silent agreement.

"Creatures like The Seventh Devil are never truly gone," Mort said, his tone becoming serious. "That's why I'm here. It was different in the old days—there was a balance, if you like. I took some, he took some…but then he needed more, and he needed them younger, before their time. In short, he got greedy. There's a gate between his world and yours, a gate that he's forced open to come and go as he pleases, much to my annoyance and to the detriment of humankind. The balance needs to be restored, the gate needs to be closed and, not that I like to brag, but I'm the only one who can help you do it."

Gareth's eyes grew wide and his jaw dropped. "You—you're *Death,*" he whispered.

I shook my head and laughed sardonically. "Death? Like, the Grim Reaper? Give me a break. You don't look anything like him."

Mort Sterven arched one eyebrow, and then snapped his fingers. Suddenly, he was wearing a long hooded robe and holding a large scythe in skeletal fingers. His face was inscrutable within the shadows of the hood. He gave a low chuckle. "Is that better? And it's *Mister* Death, or just Mort if you prefer."

I gasped and pressed my back into my seat, trying to get as far away from him as I could. "Relax," he said, and snapped his bony fingers again. The hooded figure transformed once more into the man in the expensive suit and mirrored sunglasses. "As I said, I'm not here for you. But you *do* need my help."

I looked around to see if anyone else had witnessed Mort's shocking metamorphosis, but the two boys across the aisle seemed oblivious, Jimmy engrossed in a comic book and his friend staring out the window, arms crossed, still pouting. Gareth took a moment to compose himself, then said, "So Verity was right? Berith is—?"

"Back, yes. I'll explain more after you take this call." He sounded strangely apologetic.

I looked at my phone, confused. "My phone's not—", but just then, it rang. The name 'Mitchell Cooper' jumped out at me from the display screen and I jabbed the answer button, ignoring for a moment the fact that Mort somehow knew it was going to ring. I put the phone to my ear in anticipation of hearing Mitchell's warm voice, but instead it was his ex-wife, Pascale. She was crying. I listened for a moment, then said woodenly, "We'll be there right away." I hung up and stared at Mort, my face full of anguish, angry tears beginning to form.

Gareth looked at me questioningly, already expecting the worst. "Verity?"

"That was Pascale," I answered. "Mitchell's dead."

7

STRANGERS ON A TRAIN

Gareth stared at me for a moment, speechless, then turned away, eyes closed. He clenched his fists together tightly. "How?" he whispered. His knuckles were white.

"She said—," I paused, wiping away a tear that had made its way down my cheek, the words I was about to say too horrific to contemplate. "She found him in the bathtub. He'd taken his own life."

Gareth's eyes flew open wide and his jaw dropped. "*What?*" he exclaimed, loudly enough that the boys across the aisle looked over, curious. "No," he said more quietly. "I don't believe it. Mitchell would never. Not after what he'd been through. He knew better."

"I told her we'd be there right away. She needs us."

Gareth and I had both forgotten about Mort Sterven, but then he cleared his throat. "I'm sorry for your loss," he said. "Now, as I was saying—"

"What the hell do you mean, 'as I was saying'?" I spat at him. "And if you really are Death, which I doubt, why are you here and not with all the people who are dying at this very moment?!"

Mort shifted in his seat uncomfortably. "I understand," he answered. "It was simpler in the old days, when it was just scattered tribes around the globe. But now there's over 7 billion of you—I've had to 'outsource', obviously. I'm only called in when there's a case that's not so clear-cut in terms of the, ah,...destination."

"So you don't actually know what happened to Mitchell? I can tell you without a shadow of a doubt, there's not a chance in hell that he would have killed himself." Gareth was adamant.

Mort sighed. "Fine. Give me a second." He unfolded the strange newspaper and opened it, scanning the pages. "Mitchell Cooper? Halifax?" he asked. I nodded. A moment later, his brow furrowed in perplexity.

"What does it say?" I prompted him.

He closed the paper and refolded it nine times until it was an unbelievably small size, then tucked it into the inside pocket of his suit. "It's not clear. I'll need to consult with my associate. We can continue this conversation later."

"Not clear? But we're heading out to Halifax first thing tomorrow morning—can't you tell us anything before then? This is urgent!"

"Don't worry. Once I have a better understanding of the situation, I'll find you." With that, he got up swiftly and exited through the door that joined our train car to the one behind us.

I leapt up to follow him, channelling my grief into fury. I could see him through the small window in the door—he was already at the other end of the next car, standing in the vestibule with an elderly man who was dressed eccentrically in an old-fashioned suit and a top hat. He was carrying an intricately carved white cane and wearing small round black sunglasses. Mort was leaning over and speaking into the man's ear, and as I watched them, the elderly man turned his head and looked directly at me.

The black lenses seemed to absorb the sunlight flooding the car, making his eyes appear hollow, and he suddenly gave me an eerie smile. He said something to Mort and gestured with his cane. I glanced over my shoulder at Gareth to tell him I'd be right back, but when I pushed through the door, there was no sign of either Mort or his companion. I made my way along the swaying train car, trying to keep my balance, scanning the seats for them, and then went through to the next car, doing the same. I couldn't see them anywhere. When I got to the end of the last car, I sagged against the wall of the vestibule, watching the tracks disappearing behind us around a bend, feeling defeated and helpless. I made my way back to Gareth and told him what had happened, describing the elderly man to him in detail.

"I still can't believe that was Death and his 'associate'. Probably a couple of nasty malevolents having fun at our expense."

Gareth shrugged and exhaled a long, exhausted breath. "I suppose we'll find out if we *do* see him in Halifax." He fell silent, lost in thought, then said, "Mitchell. It can't be true. Are you sure that's what Pascale said? Maybe there was something lost in translation—English isn't her first language."

"She was distraught, bordering on hysterical, but she speaks English fluently, and she was very clear about what happened. She couldn't reach him for a couple of days, went over, and found him there. She was too upset to provide any details and I didn't push her. We can get more information when we get to Halifax." My eyes started filling with tears again. "It doesn't seem real, like this is just another nightmare."

Gareth nodded in silent agreement and rested his forehead in his hands. After a minute, I realized that he was crying. I put my hand gently on his shoulder and we sat like that until we arrived at the station. Horace was there to meet us, this time with Quentin's SUV instead of the convertible. When he saw us, he smiled and waved us over, but as we got closer, his smile dropped.

"My dears, whatever is the matter?" he exclaimed. "You look like you've lost your last friend!"

I wiped my eyes and said, "Pretty close." We got in the SUV and I told Horace what had happened. He was horrified.

"Nicky Cooper's brother? The one who helped you capture that terrible man? But why?" His face was pale. Horace had never met Mitchell, but he knew all about him initially from his own research into Nicky Cooper's disappearance and then from Mitchell's work with us; learning about Mitchell's death seemed to have shaken him. Gareth was busy on his phone, booking plane tickets, so I answered.

"We don't know yet, Horace. We're flying out there first thing in the morning. I can't believe it myself, and neither can Gareth. Both of us are convinced that he would never have done something like that."

"I hope the ordeal with that awful Bell man didn't push him over the edge," Horace said sorrowfully. "Remember, he'd already had a breakdown when he was younger. Who can say what goes on in people's hearts the whole while they seem happy."

"True, but...well, there's no point in speculating until we get more information." I changed the subject, trying to distract both of us. "So when are you leaving for your honeymoon?"

Horace brightened a little. "Friday. Quentin has us booked into this lovely resort up north. Apparently, he's going to teach me how to fish...."

When we arrived at The Echo, Quentin was there to greet us. Horace took him aside and filled him in while Gareth and I went to our rooms to unpack and repack for the morning. Not long after, there was a knock on my door.

"Verity, it's Wes," he called out. "Is it okay if I come in?"

I opened the door and he was standing there, looking concerned. "Uncle Q. told me what happened to your friend. I'm really sorry."

I smiled wanly and invited him in. "I didn't know you'd still be here," I said. It felt weirdly good to see him. Even though we'd just barely met, I felt the same type of calm in his presence that I felt with Quentin.

"Oh, I took some extra time off work so that I could watch the place and help out while the uncles honeymoon up North. I'm glad you're back so soon—I wanted to tell you what I found out about Samuel Bell."

My heart started racing, and Wes must have intuited it because he immediately added, "Nothing to worry about, really. I got into Strongpoint's system and looked up his records. He's still comatose. Aside from what was listed as 'intermittent unusual brain activity', he's in the same condition as he's been for almost a year, completely unresponsive."

"But what does that mean, 'unusual brain activity'? Unusual how?" I was starting to feel a sense of dread, but Wes was quick to reassure me.

"I looked it up. Patients in comas generally have some minimal brain activity. This could simply mean that his brain was reacting to a noise in his room. It's nothing to worry about—even if he *did* wake up, he's not going anywhere. After almost a year in a coma, his muscles would be too atrophied for him to get out of bed, let alone run away and escape."

"All right," I sighed, sitting down heavily on the edge of the bed and slouching over.

Wes took the cue. "You must be completely worn out. Why don't you rest up? Dinner will be at 6—I'll text you when it's ready if you want. And if you need anything, just message me, okay?"

I nodded slightly and he left, shutting the door behind him. But as it turned out, I was too tired to sleep, so I spent the afternoon researching Death, or Mr. Death to be more precise. There were a lot of references to The Grim Reaper, but not much in the way of a modern persona, and nothing at all about an older figure who may or may not be blind. Finally, I got a notification from Wes, so I made my way downstairs. I walked into the dining room and before I had a chance to say anything, Quentin was on his feet, wrapping his arms around me in a consoling embrace.

"I'm so sorry, sweetheart," he murmured.

I struggled not to start crying again—I just let him hug me for a minute, then pulled back and said, "Thanks. I appreciate that."

Horace had gone all out, whipping up a variety of "comfort foods" to make us feel better. But despite the mashed potatoes, gravy, lasagna, pizza, ice cream, and chocolate cake, I couldn't stop thinking about Mitchell, alone at the end, my mind torn between fury that he didn't reach out to us, and the terror that his death wasn't suicide but something worse. Regardless of Wes's investigation, I couldn't help having an awful feeling that Bell was involved somehow, impossible as that seemed.

Finally, Horace, never one to be defeated, passed around rum toddies. "A cure for whatever ails you," he announced lightly, handing me a warm mug. After a couple of sips, I was starting to feel if not better, then slightly more relaxed and capable of conversation.

"Horace," I said, "have you ever heard the name 'Mort Sterven'?" Gareth's head snapped around and he gave me a warning glance. "What?" I asked innocently. I knew that Gareth had wanted to keep our meeting with the mysterious 'Mr. Death' under wraps until we knew more about him, but my research had come up empty, and Horace often had tidbits of information stored in his complex brain that no one else knew about.

Horace mused for a moment and put his mug down. "Mort Sterven, you say? No, I don't believe so. Why?"

"Oh, he was just someone we met on the train. Interesting man—middle-aged, thin, expensive suit and watch, wore mirrored sunglasses the whole time we were chatting. He had a friend with him, an elderly blind man wearing dark glasses, this crazy Victorian suit with a frilly collar and top hat, carrying a fancy white cane—," There was a sudden crash and we all jumped. Quentin had dropped his mug onto the floor and was staring at us in shock, face drained of colour.

"My goodness!" Horace exclaimed, leaping to his feet and hurrying over with a napkin to pick up the pieces of glass. "Quentin, my darling, what on earth is the matter? You look as if you've seen a ghost!"

"Small round black glasses, like lunettes?" Quentin whispered, fixated on something he saw in his mind's eye. I nodded fearfully. "Then I have," he answered.

"What do you mean, Uncle Q.?" Wes asked. "What ghost?"

Quentin gave his head a shake, coming back to reality. "It was over thirty years ago. I was a rookie, walking the beat downtown. My partner and I had just grabbed lunch, when an alarm at the bank up the street started going off. We ditched our sandwiches and ran. I'd never drawn my gun before on duty, and I was nervous. My partner was ahead of me, and just as he reached the doors to the bank, they opened, and he collided with a man who ran out carrying a knapsack in one hand and a revolver in the other. My partner fell onto the sidewalk. The man stumbled and looked around wildly, then he saw me. I pulled out my gun and yelled a warning, but suddenly there was a flash and I was lying on the ground staring up at the sky. Everything was getting darker. I couldn't feel anything at all except a floating sensation, like my body was weightless. Then there was someone standing there, looking over me. It was him, the old blind man in the top hat and black lunettes. He watched me for a while as if he was trying to decide something.

Finally, he gave me this awful grin and whispered, '*Not yet.*' Without warning, it felt like I was slammed back into the sidewalk. My chest was on fire. Turned out I'd been shot. I was in the hospital for a while and on desk duty for weeks. But I was grateful to be alive."

Horace reached around from behind Quentin and hugged him. "I knew you'd been shot a long time ago, but why didn't you ever tell me about the man?"

Quentin turned in his seat. "I always thought it was a figment of my imagination, my subconscious telling me that it wasn't my time. But now—I mean, it sounds crazy, but could he have been real? How is that possible? It was over three decades ago."

"After all the things we've experienced, I have no doubt that he could very well have been more than someone you simply imagined," Gareth offered. "Not a ghost, or a malevolent, but something in a different category altogether. If grief can take the shape of a sticky black ball, then why couldn't there be a…steampunk angel of death?"

Wes laughed and it seemed to break the tension. Horace gathered up the broken glass, and right before he went to the kitchen to throw it away, he rushed back and kissed Quentin on the top of his head. "I, for one, will be forever grateful to our eccentric friend for deciding that you were worth keeping around."

Suddenly, my blood seemed to turn to ice and I began to tremble. "What's wrong?" Wes asked.

"It just occurred to me," I said, trying to stop myself from shaking. "If the man that Quentin saw is the same person as Mort Sterven's associate, does that mean that Mort really is who he says he is?"

"Who exactly did he say he *was*?" Quentin wanted to know.

I didn't respond, overwhelmed by the revelation that we might actually have been in the presence of the Grim Reaper himself instead of a rogue spirit or malevolent, or even someone's idea of a sick joke. Gareth hesitated too, but finally answered the question. "Death. He said he was Death."

There was a stunned silence, broken by Horace. "Interesting," he said. "Mort—that's French for 'dead', isn't it? And what did he tell you his last name was? Sterven?" He looked up something on his phone. "'Sterven' is Middle English for 'starve' and also Dutch for 'to die or perish'. Sounds like it could very well have been Death himself. I've never heard him called by that particular name, but there are certainly numerous historical accounts of Death's earthly manifestation. What did he want with you?"

"Something to do with Berith." Gareth was deliberately vague. "But before we could find out more, Verity got the call that Mitchell had passed away, and he up and left. He seemed worried about something."

"What could worry Death, I wonder?" Horace chuckled lightly. "Well, let's hope none of us see him or his colleague for a very long time!"

I kept quiet about Mort's parting words, that he would find us in Halifax, and so did Gareth. No point in upsetting anyone, especially with the knowledge that Mort had hinted at, that Berith may not have been completely eradicated.

After that, we went into Horace's 'parlour' for drinks. It was an impeccably decorated room in something he called 'the Aesthetic Style', with lush wallpaper, a ceiling that he'd had custom painted, comfortable wingback chairs, and a huge fireplace. Horace and Quentin stayed with us for a while, then went up to their suite, a wing of the house separated from The Echo offices and the guest rooms, leaving Gareth and me with Wes. When it was finally just the three of us, I filled Gareth in on what Wes had discovered about Samuel Bell.

"Do you think the 'unusual brain activity' means anything?" I asked Gareth. "Wes says it's probably just a reaction to noise or people talking in his room."

"I don't know much about comas and how the brain reacts," Gareth said. "But I *do* know that, given the events of the last few days, I wouldn't dismiss it too easily. At any rate, as Wes has said, after a year of lying flat on his back, Samuel Bell won't be running any marathons."

"From what I've read, it takes months, sometimes years of rehabilitation before someone who's been in a coma for so long can function even minimally," Wes added.

"Still," Gareth wondered, "it might be a good idea to keep monitoring things, just in case."

"Sure," Wes agreed. "If he so much as opens his eyes, you'll be the first to know." But as much as I appreciated Wes's confidence, I had a feeling that if Samuel Bell ever *did* regain consciousness, he would be firmly in Berith's clutches, and it would be too late.

8

HALIFAX

Gareth and I were up at the crack of dawn the next morning. The house was still except for the faint sounds of Horace in the kitchen. We had turned down his offer to drive us to the airport; it made more sense for us to leave the truck at the Park and Fly and rent a car when we got to Halifax rather than expect him to delay his honeymoon so that he could pick us back up when we returned. Still, he insisted on sending us off with a hot breakfast, and as we were packing up the truck, he came out to the front wearing a 'Kiss The Cook' apron to let us know it was served.

"You didn't have to go to so much trouble," I said, putting my overnight bag behind the seat of the truck's cab.

"No trouble at all. This is going to be a hard day for you, so it's the least I can do. Pancakes and syrup are on the table," he beamed. Gareth nodded his thanks and went ahead into the house. I put my laptop bag on the seat, but when I turned to follow Gareth, I realized that Horace's smile had faded. He was staring at the weeping willow, its graceful fronds trailing down and swaying with the wind.

A tire, hung from one of its branches by a thick rope, moved back and forth slightly.

"Horace?"

He gave his head a shake and the smile returned. "Oh," he said airily. "I was just thinking about Mimi. This tree reminds me so much of her. Did you know, Quentin hung the tire swing on that branch for me as a wedding gift? Incredibly sweet of him."

'Mimi' was Horace's older sister, Miranda. She'd died after falling out of a willow tree on their farm when she was five. Horace had never known her when she was alive, but he'd had a loving relationship with her spirit, spending hours with her under the tree when he was a child, despite his mother's objections. His mother didn't believe in ghosts herself and felt his time would have been better spent cultivating friendships with other boys, doing what she called 'boy things' instead of playing on a tire swing with his imaginary friend. Once he left for university, she'd had the tree cut down and Mimi vanished. His mother had died not long after, and Horace never knew if she'd destroyed the tree to spite him, or because her grief was too overwhelming.

I put my arm around his shoulder, and he sighed. "You know, if I stand still for a while and squint very tightly, I can almost see her there, swinging on the tire just like she did when we were children, Grace sitting on the branch above, laughing at our antics."

"Who's Grace? I've never heard you talk about her before."

"Haven't I? Well, Grace was another spirit attached to the tree—she'd been there long before Mimi had passed away. At first, I couldn't see her myself—Mimi would simply tell me what Grace was doing or what Grace had said, but eventually, she revealed herself to me too. She was older, about 17, Mennonite, I think. She'd died decades before in a barn accident, but when the developers came in and started building on the acreage, they'd torn the barn down and she fled to the tree. And then when the tree was gone—," he paused. "Well, I just hope they're on the other side now. It makes me incredibly distraught to think of them both out there, wandering in the void without a place to call home."

I wished I could comfort him somehow, although without an earthly place to tether to, who could say where Mimi and Grace were now? But there was still a possibility that Horace's energy was strong enough to call her back, so I said, "You never know. Keep swinging on that tire, and maybe she'll find her way to you somehow."

"Very good advice, my dear, and I do love a good swing." He laughed cheekily, and we went into the house together for breakfast.

The flight was brief. Gareth fell asleep almost immediately, but I was too disturbed by everything that had happened over the last few days, and worried about what we might find when we arrived in Halifax. Mitchell's ex-wife had agreed to meet us at the house on our pretence that Mitchell had some very important files that we needed to find, although she was quite adamant that she wouldn't go in. "I can't," she said, her slightly accented voice thick with tears. "I'm having nightmares about seeing him lying there in the water, so much blood—I'll let you in, but no more than that."

I couldn't blame her; in fact, after what she'd witnessed, I was impressed that she was willing to meet with us there at all. When we pulled up to Mitchell's house in our rental car, she was sitting on the stoop, waiting. At the sight of the car, she jumped up and came swiftly down the front walkway towards us, "Thank goodness you're here," she said. "Take the keys. You can let yourself in and leave them in the mailbox when you're finished." She handed a keychain to Gareth. There were several keys, and the fob was a little metal spaceship with the words "Beam Me Up" engraved beneath it. It was so typically Mitchell, so quirky and unexpected, that I almost started to cry right there on the sidewalk, but I held it together and thanked her. "Before you go," I added, "could you just walk us through what happened in a little more detail?"

She sighed and dabbed at the corner of her eye with a tissue. "As I said, I hadn't heard from Mitchell for a few days. We're still—I mean, we *were* good friends, even though we weren't married anymore, and in the last year, we'd started having dinner a couple of times a month. We were supposed to get together earlier this week but when I tried to firm up plans, I couldn't get hold of him. I was worried—he'd had issues in the past with depression and anxiety, so I came over to the house one evening. There was no answer when I rang the bell and all the lights were off, but his car was in the driveway, so I went next door to Monsieur Garnier. Mitchell had told me once that the old gentleman had an extra key so he could water the plants in case Mitchell was away. We went in together, calling for Mitchell, but no answer. Then I saw the light from under the bathroom door..." she paused and stifled a sob. "Poor Monsieur Garnier. What a thing to have to see."

Gareth gave her a moment, then asked quietly, "Did it look like there had been any type of...disturbance?"

"What do you mean? The house looked the same as it always did. Except for—except for the knife missing from the knife block in the kitchen! Why?! Why would he do this to himself?! He was a difficult man to live with, but I still loved him, and I know he loved me—I don't understand!" She began crying again, pressing the tissue hard against her eyes, her shoulders shaking.

I put my hand on her arm, wishing I could join her in her grief. "I know this is hard," I said, "but I have to ask. Did he leave a note?"

She shook her head. "No, nothing. That's the worst thing of all," she answered. "To do this with no explanation—how could he have been so unhappy and I didn't even notice?"

There was nothing either of us could say to comfort her. Finally, she took her hands away from her eyes and straightened her back. "Just leave the keys in the mailbox when you're finished as I said, or you can bring them to the memorial tomorrow," she said brusquely. "It starts at 11."

After she was gone, Gareth and I turned our attention back to the house. It seemed fine to me, a good house, not one of the bad ones where something terrible had taken place, even though something terrible *had*. Then I had a sudden realization and I nudged Gareth. "Do you remember the first time we were here last year? The front yard had been taken over by weeds, the flowerbeds were empty, and the paint was peeling from the windowsills. I hadn't really paid attention when we were here last week, but the difference is incredible." The lawn was immaculate and had been mown not long ago, there was fresh paint on all the trim, and the flowerbeds were a riot of colour. Two baskets full of geraniums hung on either side of the front door.

"It's completely transformed," Gareth agreed. "If the outside of a man's house could reflect his current mindset, compared to a year ago...."

"It just reinforces what I've been saying. He *was* depressed when we first met him last year. Now the house looks like it belonged to someone who was genuinely happy."

Once we opened the front door, it was the same situation inside. Where once there had been chaos, with stacks of books threatening to topple over at any moment, there were now built-in bookshelves, with every volume neatly slotted. The house was immaculate, with carefully tended plants on the windowsills, and the kitchen table, where we had shared a meal so recently, was cleared off instead of cluttered with magazines, newspapers, and take-out containers the way it had been a year ago. We wandered around in silence, until Gareth finally spoke. "Do you sense anything?"

I shook my head, distraught. "Nothing. I thought...I hoped that there would be something, that I could see him again and find out the truth, but so far, the house is empty. There's only one last place to look." I'd been dreading this moment, terrified at what we might see in the bathroom, but when Gareth opened the door, it looked the same as the rest of the place, neat and tidy; the only indication that someone had ever used it was the lone toothbrush in the ceramic holder on the counter.

Gareth exhaled slowly, as if he'd been holding his breath. "I wonder who cleaned up?"

I closed my eyes and concentrated, but still, I sensed nothing. "What about you?" I asked Gareth. "Anything?" Even though Gareth wasn't able to see ghosts and spirits, he had other ways of determining their presence, including through his highly sensitive sense of smell.

He sniffed the air. "No."

We went back to the kitchen, both of us feeling bereft, let down by the absence of Mitchell. I picked up a pile of envelopes that had been neatly stacked next to the toaster and idly flipped through them. They were mostly bills that had been paid or requests for donations to various charities, but something caught my eye. "Look at this!" I exclaimed to Gareth, waving an invoice at him. "It's the receipt for those hanging baskets out front. He bought them last Saturday, two days before he died. Why would he buy something like that if he was intending on killing himself? And look—at the bottom, there's a delivery date for a tree that he'd purchased at the same time. A dwarf crab-apple, arriving *tomorrow*. None of this points to someone who was planning on taking his own life!"

"Verity," Gareth said softly. "I know you're trying to figure this out, but the things people do when they're severely depressed, suicidal even, don't always make sense. Right before my father died, he bought a dozen Bibles, gave them as gifts to the people in his congregation that he felt closest to."

I was astonished. Gareth had never once spoken about his father, a lay minister, aside from a mere mention the few times when he'd been really drunk, but even then, had never discussed his death. "You mean, your father…?"

"Hanged himself in the church vestry, yes. It was awful. I was in university at the time, hadn't seen him for years."

"I'm so sorry. I didn't know that."

Gareth shrugged. "Who can say what guilt haunted him after Julia's death? I think somehow, my father blamed himself, in the same way that Mitchell felt responsible for his brother Nicky's death, but he kept it hidden until…anyway, maybe it was the same. Maybe, Mitchell just couldn't forgive himself."

We stood there for a moment in silence. Gareth's first encounter with a malevolent, although he didn't know it at the time, had happened when his younger sister Julia had been lured into a river by John Berith. Gareth had seen her spirit for days after she drowned but had inadvertently crossed her over. He'd been tormented for years because of that, but eventually had come to realize she was in a better place. I was just about to say I honestly thought Mitchell had gotten past his guilt over Nicky's death in the same way that Gareth had resolved his feelings about Julia, when the silence was shattered by the doorbell ringing, a harsh discordant sound that made both of us jump.

I ran to the door, and as I approached it, the doorknob began to rattle as if someone was trying to get in. I could see a silhouette against the curtains. I realized with a start that whoever was standing on the front stoop was wearing what seemed to be a top hat, and I stopped dead in my tracks. "*Gareth,*" I whispered. "*I think it's the man from the train, the one who was with Mort Sterven!*"

Gareth pushed past me and pulled the curtain back slightly. "It *is* him…and Mort is right behind him."

We didn't know what to do, so we just stood there for a moment, frozen, in complete silence, then a voice rang out. "Time's a-ticking, you two. Open the door and let us in—we have something important to tell you!"

9

THE PORTEND

I hesitated and glanced over my shoulder at Gareth. He looked uncertain as well, but then he shrugged. "Maybe they really *do* know what happened to Mitchell. If they were here for either one of us, I doubt they'd be knocking."

Despite my misgivings, I grabbed the doorknob and immediately my breath caught. It was icy cold and my fingers went instantly numb. Nevertheless, I turned the knob and pulled open the door, then tucked my hand under my arm for warmth. The elderly man with the elaborate white cane stood on the stoop, his sightless eyes hidden by those black circular lenses. He said nothing; he just grinned at me. From behind him, Mort cleared his throat. "May we come in?" he asked. It seemed like a formality, but I agreed with Gareth; if Mort wanted to come in, he would, with or without my permission. I nodded and stepped aside to allow them through.

Mort looked around the room incuriously, then addressed his companion. "Interesting."

"What is?" Gareth asked, annoyed. The elderly man grinned at him, and Gareth said brusquely, "And who are you?"

Mort gave a slight laugh. "Apologies. Allow me to introduce my associate. Verity and Gareth, this is The Portend. He already knows who you are."

The man who Mort had called 'The Portend' tipped his hat and continued to grin. Seeing him up close, I realized that it was more of a sinister smile than anything borne of amusement.

"The...Portend? I saw you on the train. Nice to finally meet you," I said, my voice artificially friendly in an attempt to disguise my growing discomfort.

I was met with silence. I could tell Gareth was getting fed up, and finally, his frustration barely concealed, he directed his attention to Mort, who'd begun wandering around the room. "Doesn't he speak?"

"Not really, no. Only when necessary," Mort answered, picking up a vase and casually examining it.

"What exactly does he do then?"

"The Portend? Hmm. How can I put it?" He seemed lost in thought for a moment, then suddenly The Portend thumped his cane against the floor. Mort shook his head, his reverie broken, put the vase down, and smiled at his companion. "Good point. He suggests that you think of him as an auditor. His job is to review policies and procedures, and to verify the accuracy of scheduled...departures."

"Departures as in 'deaths'?" I asked. I was trying not to shiver—not only was my hand freezing, the icy cold had started creeping up my arm and into my chest.

"Oh dear," Mort said, coming over to regard me. "The doorknob. Most people never feel it. But you're different, obviously. Here, allow me." I held my trembling hand out, and Mort took it in his own. "Like a block of ice! This should help." He placed his other hand on top of mine, and warmth quickly spread up my arm and into my body. The shivering stopped and Mort released me. "Better?" he asked.

I started to thank him when Gareth interrupted. "Enough of this," he demanded. "On the train, you said things weren't clear, that you needed more information about Mitchell, and now you say you have something important to tell us, so get to it!"

Mort sighed and said to The Portend, "Humans. So impetuous." Again, The Portend thumped the floor with his cane. "You're right, as always. Verity, Gareth—this is a little awkward for us. I mean, it's been over 2000 years since something like this happened," he began uneasily and then paused to smooth out imperceptible wrinkles in his suit jacket, "but I'm afraid to tell you that your friend Mitchell left this plane prior to his scheduled departure."

"You mean, Mitchell didn't kill himself?! I knew it!" My eyes started to fill with tears of relief and Gareth put his arm around my shoulder.

"That's not exactly what I'm saying. It's a little more complicated than that," Mort sighed again, looking uncomfortable.

"What *are* you saying then?" Gareth looked as confused as I felt. "What happened with Mitchell?"

"It seems that there were some...extenuating circumstances. I don't have all the details, since the only one who can clarify the situation is currently on the other side. But," he added quickly, seeing the dismay on my face, "we have ways to rectify that." He whispered something to The Portend, who silently disappeared through the front door.

"Where did he go?" I asked, but Mort put up a finger and closed his eyes. I was about to say something to Gareth when suddenly it felt like all the air had been sucked out of the room and my ears popped. Then I felt a familiar presence behind me. I whirled around and Mitchell was standing in the doorway to the kitchen, seemingly as solid as he'd been while alive. He staggered to one side, dizzy and disoriented, and I ran to him, crying, "Mitchell!"

He blinked hard as if the light was hurting his eyes, but when he realized it was me, he spoke, his voice choked and hoarse. "Verity. I'm so happy to see you. And Gareth—

you're here too. There's so much you need to know." He held his arms out to me—his wrists were covered in open wounds, but I let him enfold me in a cold embrace while I sobbed against his chest.

After a minute, I collected myself and pulled away. "Tell me you didn't do this to yourself," I demanded, gesturing at the cuts on his wrists.

He dropped his gaze, not wanting to meet my eyes. "I—I had no choice," he said. My hands flew to my mouth and I groaned in disbelief. "Let me explain!" he pleaded. "Berith was here! It was the only way I could get away from him!"

The room started to spin. A wave of nausea swept over me, and I felt like I was going to pass out. Gareth rushed over just as everything went dark, grabbing me before I hit the floor. "What's going on?!" I heard him yell at Mort, frantically shaking me.

When I came back to my senses, I was sitting cross-legged on the carpet. My head was still spinning, but I struggled to get up. "It's Mitchell. He says he had no choice, that he took his own life because of Berith."

Gareth's jaw dropped. "I don't understand," he said. "How is this possible?"

"He was just about to tell me more when I fainted. I'm sorry." I sat down on the couch. Mitchell was still standing in the kitchen doorway, distressed, and I said to him, "I'm all right. Please Mitchell, what happened?"

"Point of clarification," Mort interrupted, addressing Gareth. "You can't see him? Or hear him? I thought you were some kind of 'ghost buster'."

"No," Gareth replied harshly, "I can only see a void where I assume he's standing. Sorry to disappoint you."

Mort rolled his eyes, then made a circular motion with his hand. "This should improve things." Gareth's brow furrowed and he began to say something to me when he looked towards the kitchen and gasped in awe.

"*Mitchell*!" he whispered, his eyes filling with tears. "I can see you!" He walked over and stood in front of Mitchell, who smiled sadly. "What happened to you? And how could Berith be involved when Samuel Bell is still lying comatose in a prison hospital ward?"

"I don't know," Mitchell answered. "I thought I was finally past the horror of the swamp, but the other night, I had a terrible dream, a nightmare, about being back in Greenock. I was staring out over the swamp—and suddenly Berith was there. He was smaller, less powerful, or so I thought, but when I tried to wake up, I couldn't. He reached out to me, worming his way inside my mind, taking control of me, and I struggled to resist him, but he'd possessed me before, and it made me weak. He kept repeating over and over, 'I need the boy; he is the new vessel.' He said the 'old vessel was damaged beyond repair' and he was going to use me to secure the new one. I fought against him and finally came out of the nightmare screaming, only to find that he was still inside me, still forcing me to bend to his will. I had no choice—there was nothing else I could do to escape him. I couldn't allow myself to become like Bell, torturing and killing innocent children the way he did. I had no choice," he said again, holding out his arms towards us beseechingly, the raw wounds gaping.

"Oh, Mitchell, no!" I exclaimed. "You weren't weak—don't say that." I took his hands and held them tight. "I'm so sorry we weren't here to help you."

"I'm glad you weren't," he said. "Who knows what other horrible things might have happened. But what did Berith mean, 'the boy is the new vessel'? What boy?"

"I think I might have an idea," I answered. I told him about seeing Bell at Horace and Quentin's wedding, and the nightmare I'd had when we were at the hotel in Toronto. "The woman called him Thomas. I thought it was just an awful dream, but could he be the boy that Berith was talking about?"

"It makes sense," Gareth said. "But at what point did Samuel Bell ever have a child? He wouldn't be able to tell us, of course, but with all the publicity, surely someone might have come forward."

"All the publicity…that's the most likely reason that someone *wouldn't*. Would you want to be associated with a serial killer, expose your child to that knowledge?" I asked Gareth. "The big question is, why? Why would Bell, or Berith, have a child?"

"The child you're referring to is known to us as The Vessel. He's one in a long line of Berith's progeny, a cursed existence passed down from father to son every fifty years for a millennium, each one born to serve a singular purpose—to take over when the previous Vessel is of no more use." Mort Sterven spoke for the first time since Mitchell had begun describing the events surrounding his death. We all looked at him in disbelief. Gareth was more livid than I'd ever seen him.

"You mean, you've known about this all along?!" he shouted angrily. "Our friend is dead, and you just stand there and talk about it like it's no big deal? Why the hell didn't you do something?"

"We don't interfere," Mort said simply. "Under normal circumstances. But Berith has overextended his reach. As I told you before, the balance needs to be restored, and the gateway needs to be closed. We came so close—if Mitchell had only died with Berith still inside him, The Seventh Devil would have been vanquished permanently."

I snorted derisively, in disbelief that Mort could be so callous. He shrugged and sighed impatiently, giving his watch a quick glance.

"This gateway you keep talking about?" Gareth asked, still angry. "Where is it?"

"It's the conduit between Berith's realm and yours. It exists in another dimension. Some people might call it 'hell', but that's only a metaphor. We need to close the gate before he finds the child. Although the Vessel has only reached his tenth year, it would be enough. Berith's strength will return and it will be too late."

"But I don't know where the child is, if Thomas really *is* the Vessel," I said. "The neighbourhood in my dream looked like any other neighbourhood, and the house was the most ordinary house I've ever seen. How do we find him? And how do we stop Berith from finding him first?"

"Despite everything, your friend has bought us some time," Mort assured us. "It would have taken a lot of Berith's energy in his current state to locate Mitchell and attempt to possess him. By removing himself from the equation, Mitchell forced Berith back through the gate, weaker than ever. But it won't be long before his strength returns and he might try again—maybe with one of you. And although you're only human, I've actually grown quite fond of you both. For now, however, I need to consult with The Portend." He smiled, then looked at the expensive watch on his wrist and frowned. "Time's a-ticking, Mitchell. Let's go."

"No!" I exclaimed. "Why can't he stay here? You have that power!"

Mort began to speak, but Mitchell interrupted him. "No, Verity. I don't want to stay. I'm with Nicky now, and for the first time in my…life, ironically, I've been able to let go of the guilt. Nicky never blamed me for what happened to him, I know that now. He's been alone for so long, and I want to be with him, to make up for all those decades lost between us. There's nothing here for me anymore so let me go. Please."

Gareth nodded and held out his hand. Mitchell took it and said with a smile, "Know that I'll be watching over you, even if you can't see me." Gareth stepped back; I threw my arms around Mitchell and whispered, "Who's going to do all the research now? You know Gareth hates computers."

Mitchell laughed. "I understand there might be someone who's more than happy to take my place, if the way Weston Crane looks at you is any indication."

I was just about to protest when Mort cleared his throat loudly. "I'll see you soon," he said. Then he snapped his fingers and Mitchell Cooper and Mr. Death disappeared.

10

MAGGOTY MADDY

We sat in silence for a long time, each of us distracted by everything that had just happened. Finally, Gareth sighed deeply and stood up. "We should go," he said. "There's nothing more to do here."

I nodded in silent agreement. We were locking the door behind us, about to put the key in the mailbox when a voice rang out. "Hello there!" An elderly man was making his way through a gap in the hedge that divided Mitchell's front yard from the driveway next door. He was waving to us as he walked, as if he thought we were going to vanish at any moment, and by the time he'd gotten to the stoop where we were waiting patiently, he was out of breath. He put one hand to his chest and panted, "Good morning. Is the house on the market already?"

"No. We're friends of Mitchell's. We came by to pick up some files," I answered, realizing too late that both my hands and Gareth's were empty.

The neighbour's eyes narrowed suspiciously. "Well, you can leave the key with me," he ordered, holding out his hand. "I always had the extra one so I don't mind keeping this one until his ex comes back."

"Oh, you're Monsieur—Mr. Garnier. Pascale told us that you had always watched the place for Mitchell if he was away," I said, handing him the key.

His face softened. "That's right. And I was with her when...," he paused for a second. "Anyway, I cleaned up for her. She didn't need to deal with that."

"I'm sure she appreciates it," Gareth said. "Are you going to the memorial?"

"Wasn't invited. Never mind. Better to remember him the way he was." Mr. Garnier passed a hand over his eyes, then turned and started to walk back to his house. All of a sudden, he stopped. His spine seemed to jerk as if he was a marionette that someone had yanked hard, and he whirled around with a speed I wouldn't have thought possible. His face had changed from kindly to sneering and his eyes were flashing yellow. "This is your last warning," he growled. "The Reaper and his foolish friend can't help you. Do not test me!" A roar of air rushed towards us, and just as it reached us, it gusted upwards and vanished. Mr. Garnier was blinking hard, bewildered. "What were we talking about?" he asked, his voice quavering.

"We were thanking you for taking care of the place. Have a good day," Gareth responded, his voice friendly, normal. Mr. Garnier made his way unsteadily through the hedge and disappeared into his own house.

"What the hell?!" I exclaimed, once he was gone. My hands were shaking, and I wasn't sure if it was from fear or rage. "You saw that too, right? It wasn't my imagination?"

"I saw it."

"How can you stay so calm? I thought Mort said Berith's energy was diminished, that he'd been forced back through the gate!"

"That was all bluster, no substance—a last desperate attempt, exploiting an elderly man. If Berith really wanted to hurt us, if he was truly capable of it, he would have. All these warnings are simply a cover for his weakness, and the more he threatens us, the more obviously afraid of us he is."

"I wish I had your confidence," I said. "But can we please just get out of here?"

The drive back to our hotel was brief, and we opted to eat takeout in my room, rather than venture into the city centre. We'd been in Halifax not that long ago, and neither of us had any interest in sightseeing—we were both exhausted, mentally and physically. Gareth wanted to have an early night, and after he was gone, I laid out my clothes for the memorial the next morning and watched an old black and white Western on the hotel TV, hoping that the subject matter was so far from the day's events that I might be able to get a decent night's sleep. I didn't, not so much because of any nightmares but because every time I closed my eyes, I saw Mitchell, and it made me furious to think about all he'd been through and the sacrifices he'd made for us already. It was so unfair—I kept railing about it internally until the sun began to peek over the horizon and I finally gave up on sleep. I could hear Gareth moving around in his room so I ordered room service for both of us.

When breakfast arrived, I knocked on the wall and he came over. He was already dressed in his suit, and he was carrying his laptop. He looked weary and had dark circles under his eyes.

"Didn't sleep well either?" I asked, passing him a plate of toast and a small pot of jam.

"I never thought when I bought this suit that I'd be wearing it twice in one month," he said. He put the laptop on the table. "And do you have any idea how many children named 'Thomas' there are in this country?"

I laughed sardonically. "Like trying to find a needle in a haystack. Maybe we can get Wes to cross-reference hospital birth records and school records. Unless the woman I saw in my dream gave birth at home and also homeschools her son, there has to be some way to trace him before Berith regains his strength. And when he does, what then? Berith was able to lure children away because Samuel looked so normal, so safe. Any kid I know would run screaming from something like Berith."

After breakfast, Gareth left me to get ready. I threw on a pair of dress pants and one of the few decent blouses I owned and met him at the rental car. When we got to the funeral home, an imposing century-old structure, there was a short receiving line. "So few people," I said sadly.

"The neighbour said he wasn't invited," Gareth reminded me. "Maybe Pascale wanted to keep it deliberately small, given the circumstances. All she knows is what she saw."

I knew Gareth was right, but it still made things that much worse. Mitchell had been a good, kind man—the hall should have been overflowing with mourners. We took the first two seats in the second row and after a few minutes, a chaplain came out and began the memorial by leading a prayer. I was just thinking about how Mitchell hadn't been religious at all and probably would have been amused by the incongruity of the service when something caught my eye. I sat forward slightly and squinted, frowning. Behind the minister, there was a strange figure dancing in a circle and gesturing in an exaggerated way, as if mimicking him. It appeared to be a woman, around sixty, dressed in tattered clothing, and as she spun around, something flew out of her mouth and landed in the aisle next to me. I leaned over to see what it was, and grimaced. It was a maggot, small, white, and squirming on the carpet. I poked Gareth and gestured. He glanced past me, then back at me, giving me a puzzled look, and shrugged his shoulders slightly. I tried to ignore the maggot, and the woman, for the rest of the memorial, as she danced and mocked everyone who got up to speak. Luckily, there were few, just Pascale and a couple of her family members. Pascale hadn't asked us to say anything, not that I would have expected it, considering that, to her, we were work colleagues more than friends, and the memorial was over quickly.

In the reception area, Gareth pulled me aside. "What's going on?" he asked quietly. "You seemed really distracted in there."

"The woman—she didn't appear to you too?" I asked. "I thought Mort had changed all of that."

"I guess it was just a one-off," Gareth said. "Don't worry, I'm fine with it," he added quickly, noting the disappointment on my face. "I'd rather not see them all the time, at least not the way you do, to be honest."

I described the woman, and the maggot, to him and he shuddered. "Strange! You don't normally find spirits in funeral homes. I wonder what she's doing here."

Gareth was right; it *was* unusual. Spirits normally stayed tethered to the places where they died—it would be extremely uncommon for someone to die *at* a funeral home considering the vast majority of people were already dead by the time they got to one.

"I'll ask her," I said. "She's back." Sure enough, the woman was circulating the reception room, ragged dress floating around her thin arms and legs as she made faces and mouthed along with the mourners' conversations. I waited a moment until she twirled closer to us, then whispered, "You dropped one." She stopped spinning and gazed at me expressionlessly. I pointed surreptitiously at another maggot that seemed to have wriggled out of her ear.

She bent down, picked up the maggot, and flicked it at me. Even though it wasn't actually corporeal, I leapt backwards anyway, attracting some glances from the other people in the room. The woman turned and fled into the chapel of the funeral home, and after a moment, I followed, assuring Gareth that I'd be all right.

When I entered the chapel, she was up by the lectern, waving her hands and speaking silently as if giving a speech to an invisible audience.

"Who are you?" I asked.

She cocked her head to one side defiantly. "Maddy Ferraro. You interrupted me," she answered indignantly. A maggot writhed out of her hair and landed on the lectern. She picked it up and put it in the pocket of the tattered dress.

"Sorry," I said, trying to sound sincere. "I was just wondering why you were here."

"Why shouldn't I be here?" she exclaimed, sounding annoyed. "Why are *you* here?" She started to twirl away again, but I called out, "Wait!" She stopped and glared at me. "Seriously, why are you here? Did you die here?"

"I was *murdered*!" she announced angrily. She began walking towards me, fists clenched, maggots dropping to the ground around her.

"Murdered here? When? By who?"

Suddenly her face crumpled, and her aggressive attitude subsided. "I'm not certain. It was a long time ago. I was sick, in a fever, and I fell into a deep sleep. When I woke up, I was on a metal table—a man was leaning over me with a scalpel. When my eyes opened, he just about jumped out of his skin. But then he threw the blade on the floor and wrapped his hands around my throat. 'Not another one,' he said. 'You'll ruin me!' He buried me in the furthest part of the basement, under a pile of coal and bricks, and I've been here ever since. It's so awful and boring, with people crying all the time. I wish I could just go home."

"I might be able to help," I said. "Wait here. I'll be back in a minute with my friend."

I returned to the reception room and found Gareth. "You have the box in your overnight case, don't you?" Gareth never went anywhere without the carved rosewood box that he used to help spirits cross over, and I had no doubt that he'd brought it to Halifax just in case. I filled him in about my new friend, and within minutes, we were both in the chapel with the woman. When she saw the box, she began to cry, maggots falling from her eyes and dripping down her dress.

"It's been so long," she sobbed, reaching out her hand, the nails filthy with coal dust. Gareth opened the lid of the box and she plunged her hand in without hesitation, disappearing instantly. The maggots on the floor around her began to fade until there was nothing left.

"She said she was unconscious from a fever when she was brought here," I said.

"Based on the way you described her clothes, what little there was left of them anyway, she probably died during the 1918 flu pandemic. Funeral homes were overwhelmed in some places, and I can imagine back then, they weren't as accurate when it came to making sure someone was truly dead. Still, it's pretty mercenary to kill her and then charge the family for an empty coffin."

"I'm glad we could help her. Those maggots though." I cringed at the thought of them pouring out of her like tears. "Anyway, we should get back, say goodbye to Pascale. I wish we could tell her what we know, but how could we even begin to explain it in a way that she could understand?"

We weren't flying out until the morning, so I suggested going to dinner at a local inn that was renowned for being haunted. "Why not?" I asked Gareth, who seemed averse to the idea.

"These places," he said. "99 percent of the time, it's just a publicity stunt."

"Well, maybe this will be the one time it's not. Come on," I entreated him. He reluctantly agreed, and we headed over to The Angel's Wing Inn And Tavern, getting a table for two in the back. It was an ancient-looking place, with Tudor style timbers lining the walls and ceiling, and wooden tables that had the names of hundreds of patrons carved into them over the decades. We ordered from a grubby menu that had a long history of the building on the back, including salacious details about the ghost who apparently haunted the restaurant and rooms upstairs. Gareth read the description out loud to me and laughed cynically.

"The Lady In White? Are you sensing anything? Because I'm not."

I concentrated for a minute. "Nope. Nothing except a lot of active imaginations."

The waiter who came to take our drink order saw the menus lying with the history face up and started into a spiel about the mysterious Lady In White. Gareth cut him off and ordered a beer, causing the man to sniff huffily and scurry away.

"That wasn't very nice," I admonished him.

"I'm thirsty, and I don't need to hear more nonsense about non-existent ghosts. I've had enough of the real ones for the time being," he answered brusquely, then immediately followed with, "I didn't mean to snap. It's been a rough couple of days."

"I know," I said reassuringly. But when the beer came, he drained it and immediately asked for another. Gareth wasn't a big drinker at the best of times and I was concerned. "Maybe slow down until the food comes," I suggested. He snorted, his eyes already looking a little glazed.

During dinner, he had two more beers, and he was slurring his words noticeably. When the waiter came to clear our plates, he started to order another drink, but I interrupted. "Just the bill, thanks."

Suddenly Gareth looked at the waiter intensely. "You have a lot of nerve," he said loudly. Heads turned, and people were staring. "There's no ghost here. Not by a long shot. And we should know. We're DarkWinter Direct! The only thing haunting this place is high prices and mediocre food!"

The waiter gasped and I stuttered an apology. Gareth, for his part, slammed his fist on the table and then got up unsteadily, trying to open his wallet and spilling several bills onto the table in the process. He gathered them up then stood there swaying while I paid the tab, apologizing again for the disruption, and then hustled him into a cab.

"What were you thinking?" I asked him on the ride back to the hotel. I should have been angry but I was more worried. I'd seen Gareth drunk before, but never so hostile. Usually, he got a little maudlin, told a story or two, and then fell asleep.

He hung his head in mortification. "I'm sorry, Verity, I really am. I didn't mean to embarrass you." He paused for a moment, then burst out, "But these places with their pretend ghosts—they don't know what it's like to really lose someone and then see them again, knowing that there's nothing you can do to change things. Aside from you, Mitchell was the only person who understood me. And I miss him, dammit."

I took his hand and put my head on his shoulder. "I miss him too. Now, let's get some coffee into you and sober you up. We have an early flight out in the morning and I don't need you yelling at airport security." He laughed softly and closed his eyes. I stared out the window of the cab until we reached the hotel, wondering what was going to become of us.

11

FIVE STAR REVIEW

The next morning, Gareth was subdued. I wasn't sure if it was embarrassment over his behaviour at The Angel's Wing Inn And Tavern or a wicked hangover, but either way, he barely said two words on the flight home. He just sat, drinking black coffee and staring out the window, lost in thought, until we landed in Toronto. I offered to drive the truck back to The Echo and he nodded in agreement, then fell asleep in the passenger seat the second we left the Park and Fly. Luckily, we'd just missed the tail-end of rush hour traffic and made it back home by lunch. I'd messaged Horace right before we left the airport in Toronto with our ETA as well as a couple of hints about the events in Halifax, and although I hadn't gotten a response, I was really hoping he was busily preparing one of his famous lunches, anxious to sit down and hear all about it.

But when I pulled into the circular driveway of our home base, I saw something I'd never seen before. I elbowed Gareth awake. "Huh? What? Are we there yet?" he mumbled groggily, rubbing his eyes.

"We are. And it's not good." I gestured with my chin towards the porch. Horace was standing there, arms crossed over his chest, and the look on his face could only be described as 'furious'.

Gareth shook his head to clear it and squinted. "Oh damn."

We got out of the truck, and as we did, Horace stomped down the porch stairs and stormed over to Gareth. "What in the name of all that is holy were you *thinking*?!" he exclaimed. His face was red and he was absolutely apoplectic. Quentin came out onto the porch, anxious.

Gareth winced and put one hand over his eyes to block out the sunlight as well as Horace's rage. "What's wrong?"

"*What's wrong*?!" Horace was beside himself. "The Angel's Wing Inn And Tavern is what's wrong! Their lawyer called here first thing this morning! I ask you again—what were you thinking?!"

I was taken aback. "They called here? How did they get the number?"

"It seems that after Gareth's drunken...*rant* last night, he dropped one of your business cards when he opened his wallet to pay the bill. The waiter he verbally assaulted gave it to the manager, who gave it to Randall, Randall and Associates LLP, who were quite understandably upset that their client's reputation was in tatters, thanks to DarkWinter Direct!"

By this time, Quentin had joined Horace in the driveway and had put a hand on his arm in an attempt to mollify him. Horace shrugged it off. "I'm fine, darling," he addressed Quentin calmly, then turned back to us. "What do you have to say for yourselves?"

"There was no ghost," Gareth muttered defensively.

"There rarely *is*, dear Gareth! However, discretion is the better part of valour, and you were anything *but* discreet."

"What happens now?" I asked, feeling terrible and dreading the answer.

"Now? Now you get to sit with me in my office and describe to me in excruciating detail the meal of which you partook, because the only way out of this…this litigative mess, this judicial nightmare, the only way to avoid a lawsuit, was to promise a very, *very* positive review of The Angel's Wing Inn And Tavern in the next addition of *The Echo*!"

I inwardly breathed a sigh of relief, but Gareth grumbled. "They can't sue us for saying something that doesn't exist, doesn't exist."

"They can, when the existence of such a thing was confirmed over twenty years ago by Alan Sharpovsky," Horace retorted. "And they've been riding on it ever since, creating an entire business around the ghostly Lady In White."

Gareth responded with contempt. "Alan Sharpovsky wouldn't be able to see a ghost if it kicked him in the—"

"Who's Alan Sharpovsky?" I interrupted, trying to defuse the situation. Things were getting a little too heated for my taste. Horace and Gareth stared at each other in a silent stand-off and Quentin stepped in.

"Alan Sharpovsky used to host a nationally-syndicated TV show called 'Other Worlds With Alan Sharpovsky'. He styled himself as a psychic and prognosticator. He started his career with Carnival City, then set out on his own, building a large following until he got a local cable show in Saskatchewan. He would call people out in the audience, 'read their minds' with playing card tricks and tell them what the future held for them. He would have stayed fairly obscure but on one of his shows, apparently unknown to him, there was a police officer in the audience. Suddenly, Sharpovsky went into a trance, predicted that the man would be involved in the investigation of a bank robbery, and then identified where the robbers *and* the money would be found."

"And he was right?" I asked. Gareth rolled his eyes and snorted.

"Yes, a few days later, the same police officer was called in to support a search for robbers who had held up The Royal Bank in Regina. He told the lead detective what Sharpovsky had said, and sure enough, they found the suspects exactly where Sharpovsky had predicted—an abandoned warehouse out by the airport. All the money was recovered and Sharpovsky was a hero. Of course, there were some who claimed it was a huge scam, that Sharpovsky was privy to the crime, but that was never proven, and he went on to become a national TV star."

"But how did he get involved with The Angel's Wing Inn And Tavern?"

"After a couple of years, he branched out and started doing monthly segments where he would travel to places around Canada where there were ghost-sightings. He and his crew would 'investigate' using night vision goggles, hidden cameras, all kinds of things, to determine if the location, usually a business like a hotel or restaurant was haunted. Most of the time, he claimed it was, leading to instant fame for the owners. Of course, there were rumours that he was paid off by many of them to certify the existence of a paranormal presence, but that was never proven either."

"Nobody had to prove it," Gareth stated flatly. "All you had to do was look at his mansion, his private jet, his Lamborghini—you don't make that kind of money working for a government-funded national broadcaster."

"What happened to him? Is he still on TV?" I asked.

"No," Horace answered. "Ironically, he was unable to predict his own passing, and he died in a tragic car accident in that very Lamborghini. Regardless, his reputation lives on, as will the existence of The Lady In White, if I have anything to do about it. To my office now, please. I've promised to post a five-star review by end of day."

"Well, I can't help you. I don't even remember what I ate." With that, Gareth turned his back on us and walked away. Horace watched him disappear into the house, speechless for once.

"Don't worry, Horace," I reassured him, despite my own misgivings. "I'll help you with the wordsmithing. Gareth—it's been a long couple of days, and I think Mitchell's death hit him harder than he'd like to admit. Let's get this review written, and then I'll fill you in about what happened in Halifax."

Quentin put his arm around my shoulder and gave me a fatherly squeeze. "Before you two embark on your literary journey, I think you should eat something first. I've got sandwiches ready—I know it's not a 'Horace-level' luncheon, but it'll do until later."

We sat at the kitchen table, no one saying much. I'd knocked on Gareth's door to let him know about the sandwiches, but instead of inviting me in, he texted back that he wasn't hungry, which only increased my concern. Once lunch was finished, Quentin started cleaning up while Horace led me to his office.

"All right," he said, beginning to type. "Headline: 'The Angel's Wing Inn And Tavern'. Sub-headline: 'Supernaturally Superb!' What would you say about the food, my dear?"

"To be honest, it wasn't that great. Typical pub food, really plain."

"Hmmm," Horace pondered for a moment, then spoke out loud as he typed. "'Traditionally prepared local cuisine, perfect for even the most sensitive of palates.' What else?"

I thought for a moment. "Gareth had nachos. He said they weren't as good as the ones at the Drumbo Pub."

"Let's see… 'Make sure you order the Chef's Special, the Nacho Platter. Easily compared to some of the best pubs in the country.'"

I couldn't help but laugh out loud. "Horace, I don't know about this!"

"I didn't say the nachos were *better* than some of the best pubs; I just said they could be compared. Is there anything dishonest about that?"

"Well, no but...."

"And finally, the cherry on top of the pile of manure— 'If you dare to stay overnight in one of the well-appointed rooms, be on the look out for the famous Lady In White, whose existence was once verified by well-known TV personality Alan Sharpovsky.' There. All done. I'll send it later after Quentin proofreads it for me. I don't want those lawyers having any grounds for complaint." He looked up from his computer as Quentin walked into the room. "Ah good. Now that Quentin's here, my dear Verity, what happened in Halifax?"

I started at the point where we were at Mitchell's house, describing in detail our encounter with Mort Sterven and The Portend. Quentin gasped. "There's no doubt—the man I saw when I was lying there on the sidewalk really exists? So I was 'ahead of schedule'? What does that even mean?"

"I wish I knew. But he's supposed to be very good at his...job. That's why they were so concerned about Mitchell, and why The Portend brought him back from the other side. Seeing Mitchell again was heartbreaking, and awful, but at least we got to hear what really happened. Mitchell didn't take his own life—well, he did, but only to prevent Berith from possessing him and using him to track down someone called The Vessel, apparently the son of Samuel Bell."

Horace and Quentin both stared at me wide-eyed. "I know," I said. "It's a lot to take in. And you wonder why Gareth is behaving so out-of-character? Seeing Mitchell like that was devastating to him—he told me right before we went into the house that his own father had committed suicide. This whole situation has triggered something in Gareth that I've never seen before."

Horace was perplexed. "What do you mean, 'seeing Mitchell'? I didn't think Gareth could see spirits."

"He normally can't, but Mort made it possible. It wasn't permanent, but it was long enough that he could see and talk to Mitchell as well as I could."

"Poor Gareth," Horace sighed. "No wonder he's been in such a mood. But what do we do? What are the next steps?"

"Good question," I answered. "According to Mort, Berith is too weak to try anything right now; he's retreated back through 'the gate' between his dimension and ours, in order to regain his strength. That means we have a little time to regroup. We need to find Thomas before Berith does, and we need to figure out how to close this gate for good. Mort said he was the only one who could help us do it, and I believe him, but we need to prepare ourselves. Where's Wes? I was hoping he could help out if he's got the time."

"He's just gone into town to get some groceries and supplies. He should be back any minute now and I'm sure he'll be *very* happy to see you," Quentin said with a knowing grin.

I felt my face going red, and I had no intention of admitting that I was looking forward to seeing Wes too, so I quickly changed the subject. "I'm still really worried about Gareth. He told me when he was drunk that aside from me, Mitchell was the only other person who really understood him."

Horace nodded. "Dear Gareth *is* an enigma. He must feel so lost right now. Perhaps a homecooked meal of his favourite comfort foods will help. I'm sure I have a roast in the pantry freezer...." He bustled out of the room to investigate. Quentin watched him leave, adoration in his eyes.

"That man. He thinks any problem can be solved on a full stomach, god love him."

"If only it were that easy," I smiled wanly. "I think I'll go up to my room and unpack, maybe have a shower before Wes gets back. It's been a long couple of days." I left Quentin sitting there, wishing I had a small part of his and Horace's optimism, wishing I could wash the grief from my skin as easily as eating a homecooked meal.

12

PLAN B

Once I'd finished showering and gotten changed, I went out into the hallway and stood by Gareth's door. There was no noise coming from inside—he couldn't possibly have been asleep again after the two hour nap he took in the truck, but he obviously didn't want to be disturbed. I decided to message him about the roast beef dinner that Horace was planning rather than knock. The faint chime of my text went off inside his room but there was no response. I was about to message again when I heard voices and laughter coming from downstairs. It sounded like Wes, and I was suddenly and inexplicably self-conscious. I took a quick glance at myself in the hallway mirror. My hair was still wet from the shower but otherwise I looked fine, maybe even pretty. Then I gave my head a shake and laughed derisively at myself, feeling slightly foolish. Despite Quentin's cheeky hints, I doubted very much that Wes had any special interest in me—he was just a friendly person, and probably more intrigued by our 'cleaning business' than he was by me personally.

Still, when I came downstairs to the hallway where he was carrying in bags of groceries, I couldn't help but notice that his eyes seemed to light up when he saw me. Quentin was with him, but he made a discreet and graceful exit, muttering something about putting the ice cream in the freezer before it melted.

"Verity!" Wes exclaimed cheerfully. "You're back." Then he continued more sombrely, "Did you get the answers you were looking for in Halifax?"

I filled him in as best I could, not certain exactly how much to share, or how much he was able to take in. Sure, he was aware of what Gareth and I did, but that didn't mean he could wrap his mind easily around all of it—I had no idea how much previous knowledge of the world 'beyond the veil' he already possessed. But when I was finished outlining the events in Halifax to him, he seemed to accept it all as completely normal.

"So Mort Sterven and his friend—they can help you shut the gate, but first we need to find the Vessel? I can probably help you do that, no problem," he offered.

"Really? How?"

"Well, there's this thing called the 'internet'—just kidding! There are a lot of databases out there with information in them, like say, birth records. If The Vessel is Samuel Bell's child, then I can try to find a birth certificate with him listed as the father. How old is the kid?"

"He'd be around ten years old, according to Mort. And he looked about that age in my dream."

"Okay. You said his name was Thomas, right? I'll start with the public sites first, see how far I can get. After that, I'll have to do some digging in...other places. The less you know about that, the better." I gave him a pointed look, which he ignored. "Here, can you carry these into the kitchen?" He passed me a couple of grocery bags. I shrugged inwardly and followed him down the hall. Maybe Wes's plan might end up on the wrong side of the law, but if he was able to hack into something that could help us save Thomas from the same horrible fate as his father Samuel, then it would be worth it.

I spent the rest of the afternoon writing up my report about Maggoty Maddy so Horace would at least have an article to put in *The Echo* besides his obligatory review of The Angel's Wing Inn And Tavern. Sure enough, when I went down to grab a drink before dinner, he was delighted.

"I'm going to call it 'Murder at the Mortuary'. Did you know that beginning in the Victorian era right through until embalming became standard, it was so common to accidentally bury someone alive that they had special coffins designed with bells, breathing tubes, and escape hatches? Fascinating stuff! Although I've never heard of a funeral home murdering someone who was fortunate enough to awake *prior* to burial—but in the middle of a pandemic, who knows what kinds of terrible crimes were committed? For example, there was recently a discovery of an unmarked burial ground in Pennsylvania, where victims of the influenza outbreak of 1918 were simply tossed—casket makers couldn't keep up with the demand and it's speculated that there might be over 1500 bodies buried there."

I shuddered, thinking about all the spirits who were probably still tethered to that mass grave. "Remind me never to go to Pennsylvania," I said. "I doubt Gareth and I would have the stamina to cross over that many spirits—Halifax was enough for one lifetime!"

Horace nodded in agreement. "Speaking of dear Gareth, any sign of him stirring? Dinner will be ready shortly and I've made all his favourites, right down to butter tarts for dessert."

"I'll go and find out," I offered, dreading the idea of knocking once again and getting no answer. But this time, when I called through the door, Gareth responded right away, sounding much more like his usual self. I waited in the hall, and when he appeared, his steel-gray hair was freshly combed and he had on a button-down shirt and pleated pants.

"Everything good?" I asked.

He smiled sadly. "I just needed a minute to think about things, get my head sorted—it's been a rough few days. I owe Horace an apology, I think, as well as some carefully curated culinary phrasing for our friends at Randall, Randall and Associates, LLP."

I laughed, relieved to see him back to normal. "Don't worry about that. Horace and I hammered out the review this afternoon. And you know he'll forgive you immediately if you rave about the meal he's spent the afternoon making just for you."

At the dinner table, Horace was all smiles, watching Gareth fill his plate. "Mm, Horace, this is absolutely delicious," Gareth said with his mouth full. He swallowed. "About earlier—"

Horace waved him off. "Think nothing of it. I've already forgotten about it. But if you'd really like to make it up to me…."

Horace hesitated and Gareth looked at him expectantly. "There's still the matter of that parrot, you remember? You and Verity were just about to pay it a visit last year and exorcise the poor thing when we got the call about your poltergeist friend. Well, the owners have contacted me again. Apparently, it's not only still swearing like a sailor, it's taken to spitting on people—and worse! Do you think you'd have time? I mean, I know you're up to your eyeballs with this Bell situation, but I can't imagine it would take long."

Gareth raised his eyebrows at me questioningly. "Thoughts?"

I put down my fork and turned to Wes. "You haven't made much headway with tracking down Thomas, have you?"

"Nothing yet. I'll have to try Plan B."

"All right," I said. "Polly it is. We can keep researching Mort's 'gate' on the way there, but I think we can squeeze a small exorcism in. It'll be nice to do something normal for a change."

Everyone laughed, and Quentin said, "Only the two of you would consider a demon inhabiting a parrot par for the course."

After dinner, Wes excused himself to get back to his computer, Horace and Quentin retired to their wing to watch TV, and Gareth and I went to the parlor. "Wine?" I asked, pouring myself a small glass.

Gareth groaned. "I don't want to see another glass of wine or bottle of beer for a very long time."

He made himself a cup of tea, and we sat by the fire quietly for a while. Finally, I had to ask. "Are you sure you're okay? I was really worried about you."

Gareth sighed. I thought for a second that he was going to give me the old "I'm fine, really" line but then he began to speak and everything just came pouring out. "It's hard to talk about, especially sober. It's just...I've been a stranger to so many people throughout my life. I've always had trouble making connections, probably because of what happened to Julia. When I put her in that box and she disappeared forever, I thought I would never be happy again. And I could never take the risk of getting close to someone, only to lose them—it was an experience I *couldn't* repeat. I left home, abandoned my mother to her grief and never spoke to my father again. Did you know I have a younger sister that I haven't seen since she was 12 years old? I don't know where she is, or if she's even alive. The sole romantic partnership I've ever had was in university, and I ran away from that too. You were the only person I've ever been able to sustain a relationship with, until Mitchell. He and I were alike in so many ways, but over this last year, he showed me it was possible to rise above the past, the fear and the guilt, and just be...happy finally. And now, it all seems pointless."

"It's not pointless," I insisted. "Remember what Mitchell said? He's watching over us, even when we don't know he's there. He'd want nothing more than to see you happy too. And so would I."

"I know," he smiled. "I just have to figure out how, after all this time, to stop being cynical—and afraid."

We stayed in front of the fire for a while longer, both of us lost in thought, until finally Gareth drained his teacup, stood up and yawned. "I think I'll turn in. Gotta be fresh for an avian exorcism in the morning."

I laughed. "Maybe all we need to do is give it a cracker, but I doubt it will be that easy. I'll be up soon myself."

Gareth left and I stayed by the fire for a while, thinking. I was surprised, but relieved that he'd finally opened up to me. Gareth was my rock, and if he couldn't withstand the challenges ahead, I didn't know how I could either.

In the morning, I brought my bags down to the hallway and Gareth was already there talking with Quentin. Horace stood to one side, hair disheveled, in his pajamas and dressing gown, and looking extremely distressed.

"Seems there's been a change of plans," Gareth announced.

Horace rang his hands together. "But what will I tell the parrot people? I've already put them off once—they sounded so desperate!"

"This is more important," Quentin said gently. "I'm sure the 'parrot people' will understand."

"What's going on?" I asked. "If it's not the parrot, where are we going?"

"I got a call from an old friend early this morning," Quentin said. "A group of students doing an archaeological dig in Bruce Peninsula National Park found some human remains. The police think it might be Anna Lewis."

"Anna Lewis?" Gareth gaped. "After all this time?"

"Who's Anna Lewis?" I asked. "I've never heard of her."

"Well, you wouldn't have, my dear," Horace said reassuringly. "You weren't even born when she vanished, never to be seen again."

"In 1984, Anna Lewis went to a community dance. She left the dance early because she had to work the next morning but she never arrived home. No one's seen her since. She was only 24 years old. The mystery of what happened to her was never solved, until maybe now. My friend is a former colleague," Quentin told us. "When The Swamp Killer case broke, she contacted me out of interest and I filled her in with a little bit more than was public knowledge—now don't fuss, Horace, she's a trusted friend with an open mind—at any rate, she was hoping that you and Gareth might drive up to consult before the media hordes descend on the site."

"It's in the complete opposite direction of the parrot," Horace sulked. "But yes, I suppose this *is* more important."

Gareth had already hooked up the Airstream, and the early morning sun glinted off its shiny exterior. We both loved the new trailer, especially the twin beds and a shower with actual water pressure. I threw our overnight bags into one of the overhead storage compartments, then settled into the front seat of the truck next to Gareth. His duffel bag, containing the carved rosewood box that we used to transition spirits, along with our other 'tools of the trade', was on the back seat, and I wondered if we were going to need it. "I'll call you once we find out more," I yelled to Quentin as we drove off.

"Should be there in about three and a half hours," Gareth said. "Quentin's friend arranged a campsite for us—she'll meet us there and then take us to the dig."

I spent the first hour doing some research into the Anna Lewis case and reporting back to Gareth every so often. "It says here that her brother was the last person to see her, that she decided to leave the dance early because she was starting a new job in the morning at a veterinary clinic and wanted to be well-rested. The police checked the brother out right away, but he had an alibi for the whole night—he was with his girlfriend and she confirmed it."

Gareth nodded in agreement and added, "From what I recall about the case, he took a lie detector test a few months later and passed with flying colours."

I read a little more. "It says on this website here that, in a later interview, the bartender at the dance remembered seeing her talking with—," I gasped out loud then clapped my hand over my mouth in shock.

"What?" Gareth asked, keeping his eyes on the road. "What?!" he repeated, when I didn't answer. "Who was she talking to?"

"An ordinary-looking man," I whispered. "Wearing a tan jacket and khaki pants."

13

ANNA LEWIS

Gareth braked and eased the truck and trailer over to the side of the road, slammed the gearshift into 'Park', then swivelled in his seat to face me. "Seriously? I don't remember anything about that, and even though I was only in middle school, I followed the case really carefully—it was all anyone talked about for weeks. I was a bit...obsessed with cases involving missing girls back then, hoping to get proof that would validate what I knew had happened to Julia. Let me see."

I showed him my laptop. "I found it on this site called 'In From The Cold'—they have a monthly podcast where they go back and look into cold cases. They did a feature on the Anna Lewis disappearance last year, re-interviewed witnesses and pieced together a new timeline."

"Why didn't the bartender say anything about seeing her with this man at the time of her disappearance? It would have been an important clue, maybe even have led to Samuel Bell being caught before he could kill any more children."

"Not Samuel," I reminded him. "Samuel's only in his mid-thirties—he wasn't alive at the time. But based on what Mort told us, then it could have been Samuel's father, whoever that was."

"But what would he have wanted with Anna Lewis?" Gareth wondered. "Berith is only interested in—wait, maybe that's it!"

"What's *it*?"

"Every fifty years, the Vessel…wears out, so Berith needs to get a new one. But where does he get it from? Mort said it was a curse passed down from father to son, but there has to be a mother, or multiple mothers, involved too, right? And each child has to be born within a certain time frame to ensure that there's a new Vessel who's old enough to continue stealing children to satiate Berith. According to the police investigation, Samuel Bell's foster records showed that he was the only child of a single mother when he was taken away from her because of abuse in the home. Had Samuel's father, under Berith's control, repeated a centuries old pattern by looking for a woman who could bear the next Vessel?"

"That's a solid theory," I agreed. "If the remains those students found *are* Anna Lewis—and if she's still tethered to the site, maybe she can shed some light on all of this. And her family can finally have some closure."

We got back onto the road and it wasn't long before we were pulling into the campsite where we were to meet Quentin's friend, Sergeant Cecilia Ling. We checked in, got the Airstream settled, then messaged her. Her response was immediate, as if she'd been watching her phone for hours, waiting for our signal. "She says she'll be here in fifteen minutes," I told Gareth. "And to wear good hiking shoes."

Gareth unloaded his duffel bag, checking the contents to make sure we had everything we needed, while I set out a quick lunch on a picnic table at the end of the parking lot. We'd just finished eating when a Jeep drove up. A dark-haired woman got out of the car and squinted against the bright noon sun. She shaded her eyes with her hand, then smiled in recognition. She looked young for someone with her rank, but the way she strode towards us was full of confidence.

"Verity Darkwood, Gareth Winter?" She held out her hand and shook each of ours in turn firmly. "Happy to finally meet you. Quentin has told me a lot about you both. I'm Sergeant Cecilia Ling. Are you ready to go or do you need a few minutes?"

I threw our garbage into a barrel by the picnic table and Gareth shouldered his duffel bag. "We're good," he said.

Gareth got into the passenger seat where there was more room for his long legs, and I climbed into the back, the duffel bag next to me. We followed the main road for about half an hour, sitting in silence after a few initial minutes of small talk, until finally the Sergeant spoke. "So what do you know about the Anna Lewis case, if anything?"

"Only what was in the papers at the time," Gareth answered. "She left a local dance alone and was never seen again. Must have been awful for the family." I wasn't surprised that he didn't mention our discovery about the ordinary man—it was too soon to involve the Sergeant in our speculations.

"Yes," the Sergeant replied. "I can only imagine how horrible it's been for them, never knowing what happened to her. Even now, the burial site doesn't offer much in the way of information. There's nothing but the remains of a body—the clothing rotted away years ago. Any evidence to indicate who dug the grave would be long gone by now. The forensic team has searched the area with a fine-toothed comb and come up empty-handed. And as for DNA, we can try to extract some from the bones and match it, maybe to a family member, but that's a long shot, given the time that's passed and the condition of the remains."

"Then why do you think it's Anna Lewis?" I asked.

"Two reasons. First, the age of the remains. The body has been in the ground for over thirty-five years, according to forensics and that coincides with the time of her disappearance. Second, and this is something only a few people knew, when Anna Lewis was young, she'd fallen off her bike and broken her collarbone."

"And the collarbone on this body is broken too?"

"Yes. Might be a coincidence, but the only other disappearance in this area over the last few decades was a woman named Kelli Needham, a waitress in Kincardine, and she'd never broken her collarbone. That leads us to believe..."

At that point, I'd stopped listening. I balled my hands into fists and squeezed them tight. "Kelli with an 'i'," I whispered. Gareth looked back over his shoulder at me and realization dawned on his face.

"Sorry, what?" the Sergeant asked.

I took a deep breath and shook my head. "Nothing, I was just saying how sad it was."

The Sergeant continued on, but my mind was racing too fast to listen. Kelli with an 'i': the woman Gareth and I had crossed over the night we met three years ago, at a bar in Kincardine, where I'd taken refuge after my first encounter with John Berith in his guise as Samuel Bell. She told us that she'd met a man who seemed nice, that they'd gone for a walk on the beach, and that he'd suddenly turned on her. She'd started screaming for help and he panicked, drowning her in the lake. Was she another one of Berith's potential surrogates for The Vessel?

A few minutes later, Sergeant Ling pulled off the main road and headed down a gravel laneway. "We can only go so far by car. I'll park up ahead and we'll go the rest of the way on foot. By the way, there are a couple of officers still on site, and I've told them that the two of you are 'forensic consultants'."

"And what specifically do you need us to do?" Gareth asked. I was wondering the same thing—Sergeant

Ling had said that Quentin told her a lot about us, but what *exactly* he'd told her, I wasn't sure.

The Sergeant shrugged. "To be honest, I really don't know. Walk around the site, see if you pick up any...vibes? I don't know what you call it. But just see if there's anything we've missed."

We got out of the vehicle and walked past a police cruiser, then headed down a narrow dirt path through towering trees. As we got further from the road, a hush descended over the forest, and the birdsong that had seemed so loud when we'd first entered had become subdued. The wind rustling through the leaves was the only sound, aside from our feet scraping the dirt. Sergeant Ling walked on ahead, which gave me a chance to talk to Gareth.

"The waitress," he said, leaning close to my ear and speaking quietly so that the Sergeant couldn't hear us.

"Yes. Remember what she said? About the man who killed her? Do you think...?"

"The more we find out, the less surprised I'd be if it really *was* Berith, looking for someone to bear his Vessel. If each Vessel 'wears out' after fifty years, maybe he was getting desperate—Samuel Bell's father would have been around twenty-five himself at the time, and Berith would have needed to get a successor lined up, one that would be old enough when the time came to replace him."

"Anna Lewis, Kelli Needham—how many more could there be? It's awful to even think about."

"Hopefully there'll be something at the site that will shed more light on things," Gareth said.

Sergeant Ling stopped and waited for us to catch up. "It's just over there," she pointed. About twenty yards away, among the trees, was a shadowed clearing that was cordoned off by caution tape and scattered with numbered markers. In the middle was a large open pit. I shuddered involuntarily at the thought of this being a final resting place for poor Anna Lewis, not much older than me when she disappeared. There were two other officers at the site, and one of them approached us. Sergeant Ling addressed him. "Constable Josic, these are the consultants I was telling you about. They'll need some time to look around, so why don't you and your partner go for lunch?" The officer smiled at us and nodded, then walked away and said something to his partner. The two of them headed back towards the path and quickly vanished into the forest. The Sergeant gestured. "I'll stay back here, leave the two of you to...investigate."

Gareth slung his duffel bag over his shoulder, and together, we ducked under the caution tape and made our way towards the open pit. I was keeping a careful eye out for signs of a spirit, and Gareth was sniffing the air carefully. "Anything?" I asked.

He shook his head. "Just dirt, decay, and a hint of—," he paused and sniffed again, "—lavender. Strange."

I thought about Anna Lewis, spraying on lavender perfume before the dance, and it made my heart hurt to think of it still mingling with the dirt that had been so callously thrown on her. Then something occurred to me that I hadn't really considered before. If her spirit was tethered to this spot, she must have died here rather than being killed somewhere else and brought to the site to be buried, which begged the question—how did someone, presumably Bell, lure her all the way out here?

I continued forward, staring first at the ground, then at the trees around us. Suddenly, something flitted from behind one large maple tree to a towering spruce, a blur of shape that I couldn't quite make out. I pointed and motioned for Gareth to follow me. We crept closer, trying not to make any abrupt movements. As we got nearer to the spruce tree, I held my breath in anticipation and peeked around the trunk. There was a figure there, about five feet away from me, hazy and undefined, as if I was looking at it through thick fog. I stepped out from behind the tree directly behind the figure. It stayed motionless for a moment, then it began to move away, floating seemingly above the ground. I looked back at Gareth and mouthed, "Come on." Together, we tracked the figure as it wended its way through the trees for several minutes without speaking until, abruptly, it stopped dead as if it had hit a wall. Gareth and I stopped as well, breathless with a mixture of anticipation and dread.

Slowly, the mist began to swirl and gain definition, until it became a woman, not much older than me, with long blonde hair. She was wearing a short dress with a flared skirt and a scoop neckline, and a golden butterfly pendant hung from a chain around her throat. "This is as far as I can go," she whispered. Her voice was mournful and full of longing.

"Anna? Anna Lewis?" I asked in a hushed voice.

"Am I?" she responded vaguely. "It's been so long since I heard someone say that name." She turned as if to wander away so I hurried around to face her.

"Anna, wait," I said. I knew I had to be careful. There was a good chance that she didn't realize she was dead, and the sudden knowledge of that might make her difficult to deal with, violent even. "Anna, do you know where you are?" But I needn't have worried. Her face turned dark.

"Yes, I know where I am. I'm in the place where that yellow-eyed bastard murdered me!"

I could hear Gareth breathing heavily behind me. "We were right," I told him. "It was Berith, in the guise of another man, maybe Samuel's father."

"He called himself Abel," Anna said. "He seemed nice at first, a little nervous. He bought me a drink, said I reminded him of someone named Agrippina, that he hoped I was just like her. I laughed, said I didn't know who that was, and he said I was as pretty as her. He wanted to take me for a drink with him after the dance, but I told him I was starting a new job in the morning as a receptionist at a veterinary clinic. Then he told me that his dog was sick, convinced me to meet him in the parking lot so that I could write down the number of the vet clinic for him. I thought he was kind of sweet, harmless, that it was just a ploy to get *my* number, and there were so many people around—but the next thing I knew, he shoved a cloth in my face and threw me into his car. I woke up on the back seat. We were parked on a side road somewhere and he was trying to—to force himself on me. I screamed and hit him, and then... he kept yelling that he needed a vessel, that I had to give it to him, and the more I kicked and screamed, the angrier he got, and his eyes were blazing with yellow fire. Everything went black, until I found myself in this forest with his hands around my throat. That's the last thing I remember. How long have I been here for?"

I paused, hoping that she would be able to accept what I was about to tell her. "Thirty-six years," I said softly.

"So long? My family!" Her ghostly eyes filled with iridescent tears. "They've spent all this time not knowing what happened to me?"

"I'm sorry. We're hoping to find a way to prove that the body in the grave is yours aside from them just taking our word for it. At least that way we could give your family some peace. Do you remember anything else, anything at all?"

"It was like a dream," she said faintly. "I could see myself, lying over there while I stood hidden behind a tree. The man—Abel—there was something wrong about him, like he had a split personality or something."

"What do you mean?"

"He was yelling at himself, furious, berating himself. He called himself an incompetent fool, said that another opportunity had been wasted because of his carelessness, and he was running out of time. He talked about a vessel and needing to find 'the one', but I don't know what he meant. Finally, his voice seemed to get louder, like it was coming from outside of him, filling up the forest. He screamed, 'You've left a sign! Imbecile! Take it back to the cabin and put it with the others!' And then he went over to my body and bent over it…," Anna thought for a moment. "My butterfly pendant!" she said, touching the illusory one at her throat. "He ripped it off my neck and put it in his pocket before he buried me. My parents gave it to me when I turned 18. 'Love Mom and Dad' is engraved on the back. If only you could find it, they'd know it was mine."

"The cabin." I explained to Gareth what Anna had revealed. "I don't remember anything about a butterfly pendant being found among The Swamp Killer's trophies. Do you think the police missed something?"

"They were really thorough, but who knows? This Abel could have stowed them anywhere. Everyone was so focused on the boxes for each child, and they were out in the open. Maybe no one thought to search for a secret hiding spot."

I started to reply, when, without warning, the ground began to quake.

"What's going on?" I called to Gareth. "Do you feel that too?" He nodded, grabbing onto the tree for support. I glanced back to where I could barely glimpse Sergeant Ling. She was looking at her phone, seemingly oblivious to the shaking and rumbling. "It must be coming from the other side!" I yelled, trying to keep my balance.

"I can feel the energy!" Anna exclaimed. "It's like something dark is trying to break free and surface. It's—furious!"

Then, as quickly as it began, the earthquake reduced to a low rumble and stopped. I breathed deeply. "All right," I said, addressing both Anna and Gareth. "I think our next move is to talk to Sergeant Ling, see if that pendant was catalogued, and if not, go back to the cabin in Little Egypt and try to find it for ourselves. Then we can finally give your family some closure."

"Thank you." Anna's eyes filled with ghostly tears. "But what about me? I don't want to stay here."

"Don't worry," I assured her. I motioned to the duffel bag. "Gareth—" The ground began to shake again, more violently. In the distance, Sergeant Ling still seemed unaware of what we were experiencing.

Anna looked around wildly, terrified. "It's getting stronger!"

I held on to a nearby tree, while Gareth steadied himself. Again, as suddenly as it began, the shaking stopped.

"I don't know what's going on," I said quickly. "But we need to cross Anna over before this gets any worse."

Gareth nodded. He bent down and pulled the rosewood box out of his bag. At the sight of it, Anna breathed a deep sigh and smiled. Wordlessly, Gareth opened the lid and held the box out towards her. Without hesitation, Anna put her hand inside it. Seconds later, she was gone, but as she vanished into the next world, the earthquake resumed, worse than before. Gareth and I clung to each other, sinking to the ground to avoid being thrown there like rag dolls. Finally, the quaking died away. As it did, all the birds in the forest began shrieking; flocks of them exploded out of the trees in terror, as if some terrible predator had been set loose among them. I held my hands over my ears until the cacophony faded and the forest was still again.

I struggled to my feet. Gareth was just about to speak when my phone went off, the ring tone harsh and jarring in the silence that had followed the disruption. I grabbed it from my pocket and looked at the screen. "It's Wes," I said. I put the phone to my ear.

"Verity, you're not going to believe this. Samuel Bell—he's dead!"

14

ABEL

Abel Ryan was happy.

His mother loved him, despite the fact that she'd never intended on having him. He was the result of a strange set of circumstances that she herself was never able to explain. She had gone into Winnipeg one Friday night with friends to a 'mixer', and woke up in a park, disoriented. Her clothes were wet from the night dew and her panties had been pulled down around her knees. She knew something dreadful had happened, but she didn't realize the extent of it until three weeks later when her monthly visitor was late. The only thing her friends were able to tell her about that night was the only thing she already knew—that she had taken the arm of an ordinary-looking fellow and was escorted to the dance floor, after which, he got her a glass of punch. That was the last they saw of her, and they assumed that she and the young man—they were unable to describe him, as if the more they focused on him, the less clear he became—had gone parking. They told her this nonchalantly, but whispered it to each other salaciously, unaware of the terrible fear that choked their friend's heart and soul.

Anyone who knew Bridget O'Malley, 22 year-old daughter of Irish immigrants and a good Catholic girl, would never have believed she'd give herself willingly to a stranger, and Bridget didn't believe it either. Regardless, she was in dire straits. She paced the floor for hours, sick to her stomach, on the verge of hysteria, contemplating her options. Abortion wasn't possible, and even if it was, she couldn't bring herself to do it. But single motherhood was also off the table—her parents, devout as they were, would never allow it. She would be shamed and banished somewhere to have the child, then be forced to give it up to the nuns, there was no question about that. Bridget was running out of options, sitting on the edge of her bed crying, when she had a sudden brainstorm. Bobby Ryan, a boy down the street that she'd known since kindergarten, had joined the army, finished basic training, and was leaving soon to go overseas. Bobby had been sweet on Bridget since second grade, but he wasn't really Bridget's type so nothing had ever come of it. Now though…

Bridget got to work. Her mother found her in the kitchen, wearing an apron and busily icing a cake that she had baked from scratch.

"Bridget O'Malley!" her mother exclaimed, laughing at the sight of her only child covered in flour. Bridget's hair had escaped from its bow, and the heat of the oven had caused tiny tendrils of fine baby hair to curl around her temples. "What on earth are you up to?"

Bridget smiled shyly, hoping her mother couldn't hear the tremor in her voice. "Bobby Ryan will soon be going abroad with the army, so I'm making him a cake as a farewell present. I'm taking it over this afternoon." She returned to creating swooping swirls in the frosting. Her mother arched one eyebrow but said nothing. Bobby Ryan? That was a surprise. But there was nothing wrong with him as far as Bridget's mother was concerned; he was a good Catholic boy and the army provided a stable income. She *had* heard the tremor in her daughter's voice but put it down to romantic nerves. She said a silent prayer of thanks—Bridget hadn't seemed quite herself lately, and if this was the reason why, her mother hoped for the best.

Later that afternoon, Bridget tidied her hair, put on some lipstick and her prettiest dress, and walked down the street with her cake to the Ryan house. Bobby answered the door and stared at her in amazement. "Hi Bridget, it's...uh, good to see you."

Bridget smiled her most fetching smile and held out the cake. "I made this for you. It's the least I could do, since you'll be going away so soon. I'm really going to miss you." She batted her eyes and made sure that her voice was suitably sad but flirtatious. Bobby immediately invited her in, astonished at his own good luck, and they spent until dinnertime eating cake and talking. When the sun began to lower in the sky and Bridget excused herself, Bobby did what any young man faced with the girl of his dreams bringing him a cake might do. He stopped her at the door. She looked up at him with her big green eyes as he declared his undying devotion to her. Bridget reciprocated in a charmingly shy way. It wasn't a lie—Bridget knew in her heart that if Bobby saved her from the terrible fate she had envisioned, she would be the most faithful wife that any man could ask for. When he suggested that they might marry before he was shipped overseas the next week, she agreed without hesitation. She felt her terror ebbing away, and a wave of relief replaced it.

No one was surprised when, nine months after the quick and quiet civil ceremony, little Abel was born. Bobby was out of the country by then, and his new bride held her child close to her, scrutinizing his face, hoping that he looked enough like his surrogate father that no one would question his origins.

Abel Ryan was creative.

When Abel was five years old, his stepfather Desmond bought him a paint by numbers kit. Desmond had married Abel's mother Bridget the year before, almost two years to the day that Bobby Ryan had died during a peacekeeping mission to the Congo. Desmond was a decent man who took his role as a father seriously. He worked at a local bar as an assistant manager and occasional bouncer, and while he liked a drink more than he should and he wasn't the sharpest knife in the drawer (Abel had overheard his mother say that to Grandma but he didn't know what it meant), he had a steady income. Bridget still had no interest in single motherhood, even the respectable widow type, and it wasn't hard to convince Desmond that he needed a family.

Desmond was perplexed when he went to Abel's room later. The boy was using the paints that Desmond had bought for him, but he wasn't diligently filling in the racing car that Desmond was excited to show off at work.

"Abel, what are you doing?" he asked, his temper flaring slightly at the thought of the money he'd wasted. "Remember what I told you—all the number ones are red, the number twos are yellow—"

"I know, Papa," Abel replied, not looking up from the cardboard canvas he was applying the pigments to, "but I wanted to paint this instead." He turned the board around so his stepfather could see it. Instead of a racing car, the boy had created a fiery landscape framed in the foreground by a heavy iron gate. The gate had been broken open and one side sagged on its hinges. Through the gate, there was a pathway flanked by flames that seemed to flicker in an almost realistic way.

Desmond was stunned and a little worried. "Where did you come up with something like that?" he asked suspiciously. "You weren't watching a grown-up show on television, were you?"

Abel shook his head and picked his brush back up. "I dreamed about it," he said, applying a stroke of yellow to a distant flame.

Desmond left the boy alone with his painting, half-impressed and half-disappointed. That wasn't the kind of painting he could take to work and boast about. Jesus, why couldn't the kid dream about racing cars? When he told Bridget about it later, expressing concern, she laughed. "He just has an active imagination, that's all. He probably heard my mother saying something about hell, or fire and brimstone, you know what she's like."

"Well, a kid that age should be painting trees and houses. And racing cars. Tell her to be more careful with what she says around him."

Bridget nodded and sighed, making a mental note to speak to her mother about filling Abel's head with frightening imagery. But it wasn't Abel's grandmother who had inspired him to paint the gates and the flames. The night before, he'd had a dream, and in it, he was standing in front of the gate. There was a man there too, a regular man, and he said to Abel, "Go through the gate."

Abel didn't want to, but the man took his hand. "It's fine," he said. "We'll go together." Abel tried to pull away but the man was too strong. He could feel the heat of the flames on his face and he could hear screaming in the distance. Right before he and the man stepped through the gate, Abel woke up. He wasn't scared exactly, but more curious, so he painted his dream when he had the chance, hoping to get a closer look at the world beyond the gate without having to go there with the man.

Abel continued to have strange dreams and he continued to paint what he saw. Bridget would have been more concerned if they were always awful, but they weren't; in fact, some of them were quite peaceful: a deep forest with an old wooden cabin at its heart, a swamp with fog rising from its surface, two boys playing with a striped rubber ball—Abel had certainly been blessed with talent, from where she had no idea, or at least refused to contemplate it. And he did well in school, giving her and Desmond no reason to be troubled about him. His teachers said he was polite and well-behaved, he got along with the other children, and did his chores without being asked twice. In every way except for his artistic precocity, he was a completely ordinary child.

Abel Ryan was frightened.

Abel never told his mother and stepfather when his dreams started to get worse. He was almost ten, and old enough to know that disclosing the horrific images that came to him at night would be cause for alarm. Instead, as the dreams turned to nightmares, his art became more serene. When he dreamed of a woman being strangled to death, he painted a calm lake at sunset. When he dreamed of a child being thrown into a swamp, he painted mountains tall enough to touch the clouds. He never told anyone, not his mother, and certainly not his stepfather who he'd heard once exclaim about a problematic co-worker, "That guy's out of his mind! He needs to get his head shrunk." Abel didn't know if he was going crazy himself, but the thought of having his head shrunk sounded scary and painful.

One Friday night, Abel was sitting in the living room watching a rerun of *The Seventh Voyage of Sinbad*. They'd eaten dinner, and Bridget was cleaning up while Desmond got ready to go to work at the bar. Suddenly, the doorbell rang, an unusual disruption to normalcy. Abel ignored it, having no intention of missing his favourite scene, the one with the skeleton warriors. It rang again. Bridget bustled through the living room, sighing and drying her hands on a tea towel, and peeked out the window to see who on earth could be at their door on a Friday night at dinnertime. Her shoulders stiffened. "Abel. Go upstairs to your room. No arguing."

Abel protested anyway, but she turned and gave him a look that he'd never seen before, a mixture of rage and terror. He scurried upstairs as she called out for Desmond. Something about her voice prompted Desmond to come thundering downstairs. They had a quick, hushed conversation. Abel knew this, because despite being told to go to his room, his curiosity got the better of him, and he sat hidden in the shadows of the dark upper stairwell, peering through the balusters. Desmond opened the door while Bridget fled to the kitchen.

A man stepped into the front entryway. He was non-descript, ordinary, wearing a tan jacket and khaki pants. He looked past Desmond at the interior of the house, as if appraising it.

"What the hell do you want?" Desmond demanded. Abel was confused. Did Desmond know the man? And why was his stepfather so angry?

"Where is he?" the man asked, ignoring Desmond's imposing demeanour.

"He's nothing to you. Get out." Desmond moved forward, ready to strongarm the stranger the way he did numerous belligerent drunks, but the man held his ground.

"I want to see him."

"No. He's happy here. He's—"

"Happy?" the man interrupted. His brow furrowed. He looked up towards the top of the stairs where Abel huddled in the dark. The man's eyes seemed to flash yellow, as if they had caught the glare of the overhead light, and Abel had a sudden faint memory about seeing the man before, but where, he couldn't remember. "Well, that won't do," the man said to himself, ignoring the fact that Desmond was towering over him, incensed, his large hands balled up into fists.

"You have no right to come here like this. How the hell did you even find us?" Desmond was on the verge of yelling, barely controlling his anger. "You know what, it doesn't matter. I've been polite, only because I don't want a murder charge hanging over my head. But I know what you did, and if you don't leave right now, I can't be responsible for what happens next."

The man looked up at Desmond and began to laugh, a dark sound that seemed to seep out of him and float up the stairs. There was liquid growl under the sound that sent shivers through Abel, and he scooted back towards the wall, away from it. At the same time, the man turned his back on Desmond, but before leaving the house, he said something that Abel couldn't make out, something that made Desmond shove him roughly through the door and onto the street, then he slammed the door and leaned back against it, breathing hard, fists still clenched. Bridget appeared from the kitchen, holding her hand out to him, but he pushed it aside and headed for the stairs. "I have to get ready for work. I'm late," he muttered, leaving her standing there in tears. Abel scurried away into the safety of his room, where he stayed alone, reading, until his eyes closed and he began to dream.

This dream was the worst one yet. In it, Abel could see himself as if looking into a mirror, but the reflection was something out of a horror movie. His eyes were stitched shut with coarse thread, the holes tearing into the flesh of his eyelids as he tried to open them. He wanted to scream but his mouth was sewn shut too, black thread criss-crossing his lips and rendering him speechless. His hands clawed at the stitches, trying to rip them away, but the more he tried, the more he mutilated himself, the blood from his torn skin pouring down his cheeks and chin. Finally, a sound broke through into the nightmare and he woke up to find his face covered in scratches. The sound was his mother, frantically talking to someone downstairs. It was four o'clock in the morning—was the man back?

But when he went down to the kitchen, he realized his mother was on the phone. "It's not like him!" she cried into the receiver. "I wouldn't have bothered you if it wasn't an emergency, but where could he be?!"

Desmond hadn't come home from work. At 2 am, she'd called the bar, but it was closed and no one answered.

At 3 am, she called the manager in a panic. He told her that Desmond had left at closing time and he had no idea where he went after that. And now, at 4 am, she was on the phone with the police. Desmond had vanished and Bridget was devastated. For three days, she sat at the kitchen table, chain-smoking and waiting for the phone to ring. On the fourth day, two police officers came to the door, a man and a woman. When Bridget saw the female officer, she collapsed onto the floor, knowing what it meant. Desmond's car had been found that morning abandoned at the side of Highway 2, and a search of the area led to the discovery of his body, beaten to death and thrown into the ditch.

"Was your husband a violent man? Did he have any enemies?" the male officer asked while the female constable held Bridget in her arms as she wept. Bridget shook her head, sobbing into the constable's jacket. But Abel knew who the enemy was.

Abel Ryan was invisible.

After Desmond's death, Bridget was lost. She began to drink, and Abel tiptoed around the house, afraid of incurring her wrath. She seemed to blame him for what had happened to his Papa, and there was nothing Abel could do about that except shrink smaller and smaller until she stopped noticing him. Eventually, she got a life insurance settlement for Desmond's death, and she used that to move far away from Parkdale, across the Ontario border to Thunder Bay. Her drinking got worse, and she started bringing home a string of 'boyfriends', unsavory men who used her, and who sometimes looked at Abel in the way no man should look at a young boy. By the age of fourteen, Abel was able to make himself disappear so well that most of the men forgot that he existed, if they ever knew he did in the first place. But not all of them. He tried to tell his mother but she wouldn't believe him, and he was helpless. He stopped going to school most of the time, and failed all of his classes, opting to hide in his room, reading horror novels, the more violent the better. His nightmares hadn't changed, but he wasn't bothered by them anymore; they were a welcome relief from an existence that he hated.

One night, his mother brought home a new 'boy-friend', a man who introduced himself with an insidious wink as Scott, a pale, chubby man whose lips were licked raw, and who looked at him the way some of the other men did, like a starving vulture looking for bones to pick. Abel shrank into his invisible place and fell asleep. While he slept, he dreamed about the dark iron gates again, the hell-fire gates that he'd first painted when he was five. The regular man was there with him again too, and he realized with a sudden shock that it was the same man who had come to the house the night his stepfather had disappeared. But this time when the man took Abel's hand and said, "Come with me," Abel didn't hesitate. They went through the gate together, and as they walked towards the flames, the man whispered, "You are Abel Bell now. You are strong. You have nothing to fear. Kill them. Kill them both."

Abel woke up and crept to the kitchen, then back to his room, feigning sleep until he heard the slow creak of his bedroom door. He opened his eyes and saw his mother's new boyfriend standing over him, licking his raw lips and staring. Abel reached under his pillow and pulled out the knife that he had secreted there. Scott's eyes grew wide and he started to back away, but Abel leapt towards him, silently thrusting the blade into the man's stomach then carving upwards until his hands were drenched with blood and the man had collapsed onto the ground moaning. Abel watched impassively until the moaning stopped, then he stepped over the body and made his way to his mother's room.

Abel Bell was a monster.

15

A SMALL WORLD

"Dead?!" I exclaimed.

Gareth mouthed "Who's dead?", his eyes full of dread, not surprising, since the last time I'd gotten a call like this, it was about Mitchell.

"Hang on, Wes." I took the phone away from my ear. "It's Samuel Bell. Wes says he's dead."

Gareth was incredulous. I put Wes on speakerphone. "When? How do you know?"

"A couple of weeks ago, I managed to infiltrate a Swamp Killer watch group called 'The Bell Ringers'—they're people who believe Samuel Bell should have been left to die for his crimes instead of being kept alive in the psychiatric hospital. There's a lot of hate, and a lot of conspiracy theories; some of the members even believe that he didn't act alone, that he was a patsy for the Eli Trask foundation, you know, that creepy right-wing billionaire? Anyway, The Bell Ringers have an inside member who actually works at Strongpoint, and this person messaged everyone in the group about 45 minutes ago that Bell had died. There's a lot of rejoicing in the chat right now. It hasn't been leaked to the press yet, but I'm sure it won't be long."

Gareth walked a few feet away and stood staring at the ground, stunned, the heel of one palm pressed hard against his forehead. "Wow," I said to Wes. "This is a lot to process. We're just finishing up here. Keep monitoring the chat group and media sites, and I'll call you later. Thanks for…letting us know." I hung up and breathed in deeply, my mind spinning. "The man who killed my sister is dead. I'm not sure what to say or how to even feel about this."

Gareth's arm dropped to his side and he nodded in sympathy. "I suppose it depends on how you perceive Samuel Bell. Innocent victim or willing participant?"

"From the way he reacted once John Berith abandoned him, I'd say the former. But it was still Samuel Bell's hands that stole Harmony from me, his hands that choked the life out of her. Even if he wasn't acting of his own volition, I can't help but despise him, with better reason than The Bell Ringers. I just don't know if his death represents some kind of justice—for anyone."

Gareth looked up to the sky. The tops of the trees were waving gently and the only sound was the rustling of leaves. The forest was as quiet as it was when all the birds had fled. "I wonder," he mused. "Those earth tremors—they would have happened not long after Bell died. Coincidence?"

"Anna said it felt to her like some terrible energy, full of rage, was trying to break free. What if it *was* Bell? And what does that mean in terms of our battle with Berith?"

"You mean 'who's side is he on?'," Gareth answered. "He could be The Seventh Devil's saviour—or his worst enemy. But for now, we need to get to the cabin and resolve this for Anna's family."

Sergeant Ling looked up from her phone as we approached. "Well?" she asked hopefully. "Was there anything that might help us with the case?"

Gareth and I both hesitated. "There was…something, Sergeant Ling," I said. "But we need to know that we can be candid with you."

"Absolutely. I've had a few encounters with strange things myself over the years, and Quentin has told me a bit—a lot in fact—about what DarkWinter Direct does. Consider my mind completely open. And please, call me Cecilia."

"First, the body in the ground *is* Anna Lewis," I began.

"I knew it!" Cecilia punched her fist into her palm triumphantly. "But can we prove it?"

"I believe so," Gareth replied. "Do you remember the Samuel Bell case?"

"The Swamp Killer? What does he have to do with this? I thought he only killed children."

"That's what we thought too," I said. "But Anna Lewis enlightened us. We'll tell you everything, but first we need you to do something really important. Can you find out if a gold butterfly pendant on a gold chain was catalogued as part of the trophies taken from the Bell cabin in Little Egypt?"

"The necklace Anna Lewis was wearing when she disappeared? Yes, I can make some calls right away. It might take a while to track the files down, so why don't you go back to the campsite? I'll find out what I can, and swing by later with some take-out from town. Chicken wings and nachos all right?"

Gareth's eyes lit up and I suppressed a laugh. Gareth was extremely thin and never had much of an appetite at the best of times, but he could put away chicken wings and nachos like no one I'd ever seen, especially after a long workday involving crossing over a spirit.

Cecilia dropped us off at the campsite, promising to return around 5 pm with whatever news she had and dinner. I could tell during the ride back that she was bursting to ask us more questions but she didn't. I admired her restraint. I spent the next couple of hours searching online for any mention of Samuel Bell's demise while Gareth napped.

Finally, around 4 pm, one of the major national networks posted 'breaking news'. I read it quickly, and I was just about to wake up Gareth when my phone rang. It was my father.

"Did you hear?" he asked breathlessly. I couldn't tell if he was excited or upset.

"Yes. It happened a few hours ago."

"Well, I hope he goes straight to hell! Harmony—" His voice broke, not with excitement but devastation, as if he was reliving everything all over again.

I let him sob for a minute, then said softly, "I know. Dad…are you going to be all right? Do you want me to come?"

He sniffed and gave a small laugh. "You're too good to me. No, I'm fine. I just wanted to make sure you knew, and if you did, that you were handling it okay."

We chatted for a few minutes more, staying away from the topic of Samuel Bell, then we said goodbye. Almost immediately, my phone rang again, a number I didn't recognize, so I let it go to voicemail. Then it rang again. And it kept ringing, so loudly and often that Gareth woke up of his own accord. We recognized the numbers of several prominent news outlets and individual reporters, all trying to get a comment from DarkWinter Direct, according to the messages. I didn't respond to any of them. I was having terrible flashbacks from the last time Gareth and I had been so much in demand, and he agreed with me that we should lay low for the time being and monitor the news sites for updates. But there wasn't any fresh information, aside from what we already knew—that Samuel Bell was dead—so I called Wes. He answered right away, and the familiarity of his voice seemed to banish the anxiety I was feeling.

"Uncle H.'s phone's been ringing off the hook. I'm sure it's the same for you," he said.

"Non-stop, and I hope he's not answering either. But from what I can tell, no one seems to have a lot of details. Anything new from The Bell Ringers?"

"Ooh, you're going to love this," he said. "First they were claiming that he was murdered by Eli Trask. Once that died down, the source inside Strongpoint came on, very freaked out. According to her, he willed himself dead, and the moment he passed, there was a power surge; all the lights in the hospital flickered, and some of the ones on his floor blew out, like completely exploded."

"Bizarre. But *willed* himself dead? How? He was in a coma."

"The details are a little vague right now, but the source seems to think that he forced his own heart to stop. I'm trying to get into the medical records, see if there's anything more specific—or unusual—about his last couple of days. What about you and Gareth?"

"It's been interesting," I said, quickly filling him in on the events of the afternoon. "Gareth and I are meeting up with Cecilia in a little bit—in fact, I see her coming now. I hope she has the answers we need—and the nachos." I smirked at Gareth, who rolled his eyes.

"You make it sound like I'm obsessed with pub food," he said, mock-defensively after I'd hung up.

"'Obsessed' may be overstating it, but you have to admit you have a thing for nachos and wings."

"Fair enough," he acquiesced. "I hope she got extra cheese on the nachos. I'm starving."

Luckily for everyone, there was plenty of cheese on the nachos. Cecilia set out the food and put a six-pack of soda cans on the picnic table, talking excitedly. "Okay, so here's what I found out. There's no record of a butterfly necklace in the evidence seized at the cabin—but even more importantly, Samuel Bell is dead!" She paused, waiting expectantly for our reaction.

"We know," Gareth answered calmly, reaching for a paper plate. "The DarkWinter Direct phone line's been ringing all afternoon, reporters wanting comments from us. We haven't responded, of course. Any word on the cause of death?" he asked innocently.

"Heart failure, apparently. I don't know much more than that. It's so strange. Up until yesterday, his heart was fine—well, fine for someone in a coma at least. I suppose we'll know more once the medical examiner is done with the body. In such a high profile case, an autopsy is certain."

"The other thing that's certain is that we need to go to Samuel Bell's cabin," Gareth affirmed. "If there was no butterfly necklace found at the scene already, it must still be in there somewhere, probably in a secret hiding spot. Anna Lewis was adamant about it."

"But what does Samuel Bell have to do with her death?" Cecilia asked. "He wasn't even born when she disappeared."

"No, but his father Abel owned the cabin before Samuel. From what Anna told us, we're fairly certain *he's* the one who killed her—and took the necklace," I said. "We just have to prove it by finding his trophies."

Cecilia was stunned. "So the rumours about it being some kind of psychosis passed down from father to son are true? That's incredible. And horrifying!"

We sat in silence for a while, eating. I was lost in thought, still wondering how someone in a coma could compel himself to die when Cecilia drained her drink and asked, "So. What's the weirdest case you've ever worked on?"

Without hesitation, Gareth and I answered in unison, "Demon cat." We both laughed at the surprised look on Cecilia's face.

"It was a minor malevolent—what some people would call a demon—who'd possessed a cat and had taken control over a woman's cat colony," I explained. "But that's not the weirdest part. Its voice sounded exactly like James Mason."

"James Mason? You mean the English actor? I wish I'd been there to hear it for myself!" Cecilia shook her head, chuckling.

"What about you?" Gareth asked. "What happened to 'open your mind' to the point where you have no issue believing that we spoke to Anna Lewis from beyond the grave?"

Cecilia cracked open the tab on another can of soda and took a large swig. "Mm. Well, it goes back to early in my career. One of my first cases as a junior Sergeant. Maybe you've heard of the Tia Dawson case?"

Gareth thought for a minute. "It sounds familiar. Wasn't that the case where the killer had kept ID cards belonging to the victims?"

"That's right, but there's a lot more to it. About fifteen years ago, the body of a young woman, Tia Dawson, was found in an alley. Her wallet was missing, so at first, everyone assumed it was a robbery gone bad. Then three more women over the next two years were discovered dead under similar circumstances, leading us to conclude that they might all have been killed by the same perpetrator. But in the absence of any forensic evidence, the cases remained unsolved, that is until I got a phone message from someone called Janine Grise. She was a retired schoolteacher who'd called the precinct several times, claiming she had evidence that could solve the Dawson murder. The desk sergeant dismissed her as a wingnut, until finally, someone passed her messages along to me. I went to her house and she told me this hard-to-believe story, that she'd bought a leather wallet from a thrift store in Elliot Lake where she'd retired, and that night, as she'd started to transfer her credit cards and ID into it, the spirit of Tia Dawson appeared to her."

Cecilia paused, looking at us as if she expected us to scoff. But both Gareth and I had seen and heard crazier things—Gareth simply took a sip of beer and asked, "Why her?"

"Apparently, Janine Grise had taught Tia Dawson at a high school in Parry Sound where they'd both lived. Small world, right? And Tia—or her spirit at least—told

Janine that she had been killed by a man named Aubrey Hanson, who'd kept some souvenirs of his kill, her driver's licence and student card, then donated the wallet along with some other stuff far enough away to cover his tracks. But, she said, Tia told her that the trophies were in the bottom of a dresser in Aubrey's bedroom. I didn't know what to think, but the teacher was so sincere that I knew I had to look into it. And sure enough, when we ran the wallet through forensics, Tia's *and* Aubrey's fingerprints showed up."

"But how did you have his fingerprints on record?" I asked.

"Good question," Cecilia nodded. "About five years before Tia was killed, Aubrey was arrested for a domestic dispute involving his mother. Eventually, she dropped the charges, but his fingerprints stayed on file. She died not long after that herself, a victim of a mugging, or so it seemed. No one ever thought to question it. But after finding all of this out, I went to my S.O. and we got a warrant to search Aubrey's house."

"And you found the ID exactly where Janine Grise told you it would be?"

"Yep. Along with credit cards, student cards, library cards, and driver's licenses belonging to several other victims—including his own mother. Once he realized that he was done for, it didn't take long for Aubrey to confess to everything. All thanks to Janine Grise and her ghostly former student."

"Wow," I said. "It really is a small world. Horace would love that story. I wonder how he missed it?"

"Oh, we kept a lid on the 'supernatural' aspect of the case. And I know I can count on you to keep it confidential. Just like I'm not going to tell anyone that we're going to Samuel Bell's cabin tomorrow—at least until we know whether or not his father actually did have something to do with Anna Lewis's death. And then I'll have to think of a story to cover up how we *really* figured the whole mystery out."

We sat for a little while longer as the sun started to go down, listening to the crickets and thinking our own thoughts. Finally, Cecilia stood up and stretched. "Well, I'd better go. Get a good night's sleep and I'll meet you at the cabin in the woods at 10 am. It's still considered a crime scene, so if you get there before me, just wait—there might be some renewed interest in the site now that Bell's dead. I'll help you navigate."

After she'd gone, Gareth and I mulled over what she'd told us. "How many times do you think a crime has actually been solved due to something from beyond the veil?" he wondered.

"Who can say? Remember all the spin that happened with The Swamp Killer? No one would ever suspect that it was all about a super-demon, his 'Vessel', and spiritual immortality, let alone believe it if they knew. And probably better that way," I laughed. "Otherwise, we'd never get any peace at all."

I said goodnight, leaving him there at the picnic table, and got ready for bed. I was exhausted too, and it wasn't long before my eyes closed. Suddenly, I was back in the woods by the Greenock Swamp. I could see Bell's cabin through the trees, and I was overcome with terror, remembering the last time I'd been there. Then I felt a small hand take mine. I looked down and saw Harmony, as clear as she'd been on the day we'd confronted Berith, her big blue eyes looking up at me. "Be careful, Veevee," she said. "The bad man is getting stronger. You need to save Thomas."

"If I do, he'll hurt you."

"The bad man can't hurt me anymore. Save Thomas."

"But I don't know where he is."

"Look for the sleeping giant. Thomas says he can see it from his house." She squeezed my hand and then let go, her figure transforming into a white whisp that disappeared into the wind, gone once again.

16

THE CABIN IN THE WOODS

"I know how to find Thomas," I announced to Gareth first thing in the morning. I'd decided not to wake him up after seeing Harmony in my dream—I knew he was exhausted from the day before, and there was nothing we could do at 3 am anyway. But the second his eyes opened, I couldn't wait to tell him.

He rubbed his eyes and yawned. "Sorry, what?" he asked sleepily.

"Thomas—The Vessel! Harmony came to me last night in a dream and told me to look for the sleeping giant, that we would find Thomas within sight of it. So you know what that means, right?"

Gareth thought for a second. "Thunder Bay?"

"It's got to be. The Sleeping Giant is one of the best-known landmarks in the province. What else could she be talking about?"

"I agree. There's only one problem. Thunder Bay is a pretty big city and you can see The Sleeping Giant from a lot of different places, if I remember correctly. It's been a while since I lived there."

"You lived in Thunder Bay?" I was continually surprised at how little I knew about Gareth. Even though we'd spent the last few years being virtually inseparable, he was always close-mouthed about his past.

"For a while," he replied. "I worked in one of the amethyst mines up there. Great city. Lots of quiet spaces to think, and I was at a point in my life where I needed that." Gareth yawned again and stretched. "Why don't you get hold of Wes, see if he can narrow his search to the Thunder Bay area? In the meantime, toss me a granola bar. We need to get on the road if we're meeting Cecilia at the cabin by 10."

I called Wes, letting him know that we had good information about The Vessel's potential location. "I can try school records," he said. "There can't be too many Toms or Tommys or Thomases around that age in Thunder Bay. I'll keep you posted."

We left the campground in good time. The trip to the cabin would take less than two hours but the nearer we got, the more the memories that I'd tried so hard to forget started forcing their way through. I focused on the scenery rushing by, but flashing images of the horrors of our confrontation with Berith in the woods kept popping unbidden into my mind—Samuel Bell driving towards us like a maniac then crashing into a tree, Mitchell being possessed by Berith and cutting his wrist to sacrifice himself and save us, Gareth battling the demon, and the explosion that we *thought* had destroyed The Seventh Devil for good. And through it all, my sweet Harmony, always by my side, until that awful moment I had to let her go forever. I could feel the panic building, and I started to shake.

"Hey," Gareth said softly, easing the truck and trailer over to the side of the road. "What's going on? Panic attack?"

I nodded, trying not to hyperventilate, my eyes filling with tears. "I thought I was done with these. Apparently not. I'm sorry." I wiped my eyes with the heels of my palms, embarrassed.

"Sorry for what? For going through everything you've had to deal with? For always being the strong one? You carry all of us—especially me. So there's nothing to be sorry for, no reason to be embarrassed if, for once, you need a moment. Now just breathe. Remember, in through the nose, out through the mouth."

I focused on breathing until I was feeling more calm. "Thanks. I just kept seeing—well, you know." I was worried if I got any more specific, the panic would start again, but Gareth understood.

"I see it too sometimes. But then I remember that we did what needed to be done that day, and if we hadn't, more children could have died. When we get to Little Egypt, do you want to stay in the truck? You don't have to come to the cabin if you're not feeling up to it."

"Not a chance!" I exclaimed. "There's so much at stake—for Anna Lewis's family, and who knows what else we might find. This is too important." Gareth gave me a skeptical look. "Really," I protested. "I'm fine, see?" I held out my hand and it was steady.

"All right," he agreed. "But if you start feeling worse, let me know."

We finally arrived and parked on the shoulder by the marker that read 4522912. The sign bearing the number was faded, and the metal post was bent sideways as if someone had tried to force it out of the ground. An overgrown gravel driveway led back through the trees, bending around a corner and disappearing. Almost immediately, Cecilia's Jeep pulled up behind us. She opened the driver's side door then stood next to her vehicle for a moment, looking out over the swamp on the other side of the road, squinting against the morning light. We walked over to meet her—I was actively avoiding looking at the swamp, remembering all those small bones that had been hidden within its depths. As we approached, Cecilia held up a hand in greeting.

"Seems pretty quiet here so far. Let's get in and done before the media hordes arrive."

We followed her down the driveway. Once again, as the trees closed in, a vacuum of silence seemed to engulf us, waiting, threatening somehow. I shook off the feeling of dread as we got closer to the cabin. There was the tree that Samuel Bell had crashed into, the large gash in its trunk looking as fresh as if it had happened yesterday, and the scorch marks were still visible on the ground from that last battle with Berith. I shuddered and Gareth glanced over at me, concerned. I gave him a brave smile and carried on. When we came to the spot where Berith, in the guise of Gareth's baby sister Julia, had appeared in a last-ditch attempt to kill us, we both paused. Gareth breathed in sharply, and I reached out and took his hand, giving it a squeeze of reassurance. This was as hard on him as it was on me, I realized; Gareth carried me as much as I carried him, and I wished he would give himself more credit for his own strength. Cecilia must have sensed our trepidation, because she looked back.

"Everything okay? I didn't think about how disturbing this must be for both of you, coming back to the scene like this."

"We're fine," I smiled, letting go of Gareth's hand. He gestured 'after you' with a grin of his own, and we mounted the steps of the cabin's front porch. There was still weatherworn crime scene tape across the doorway and I hesitated.

"Don't worry," Cecilia said. She tore down the tape. "Ready?"

I swallowed hard as she opened the door. Stale air hit me in the face—air that had been trapped inside the tiny structure for over a year. It smelled like old wood, with a darker musty odour underneath. Gareth crinkled his nose in disgust; his sense of smell was finely tuned and much more sensitive than mine, so if it bothered me, I could only imagine how Gareth felt. We all stepped inside and I scanned the dim interior. It was sparse, barren; the person who had inhabited the space had no attachments, no sentimentality.

What could have been a peaceful haven in the forest was simply a utilitarian setting for horrors. It had remained unchanged from the day the police had cleared it out, with a wooden table and a single chair, a twin sized bed, and a small worn couch and coffee table. There were two doors: one led to a cramped washroom, and the other, standing wide open, was the closet where the police had found the boxes, neatly labeled with the names of the children Bell and his murderous lineage had killed to sustain Berith.

I'd never been inside the cabin before, but despite the closet being completely empty now, I could still see those boxes in my mind's eye as I imagined them—Nicky, Melody, Arjun, Curtis, Mary, Lorena, Johannes, and so many more, representing such loss and grief that it was almost palpable. And finally, Harmony. I knew what was in her box and I forced myself not to think about the tiny T-shirt, the words 'Powered by Sparkles and Glitter' shining rainbow bright above a sequined unicorn. I inhaled quietly and held the air in my lungs until I was dizzy, knowing that if I breathed, I would break. While I stood there frozen, Gareth was walking the perimeter of the small interior, sniffing, his nose on high alert. Cecilia leaned against the kitchen counter that stood between an ancient refrigerator and stove.

"As you can tell, there aren't many hiding places here," she said, gesturing at the empty space. "And it didn't appear as if Bell was trying to conceal any evidence. The trophy boxes were all just stacked in the closet for anyone to see."

Gareth didn't respond but continued wandering around the cabin. I stayed in the corner of the room, watching, trying to discern any foreboding presence but there was nothing unusual. Then Gareth paused by the couch, running his index finger along its arm gently. Suddenly, he grabbed it and pulled it away from the wall. Cecilia and I both jumped, startled.

"Did anyone look under here?" Gareth asked mildly.

"Of course," Cecilia responded. "There was nothing under the couch."

"I meant 'under the floorboards'. There's a faint but distinct scent of lavender wafting up through them."

Cecilia went over to the couch and sniffed, perplexed. "I don't smell anything at all," she said. "Just mildew and dust."

Gareth knelt down and peered closely at the floor. "These two boards seem slightly further apart than the rest." It was almost imperceptible, but when I examined it as well, I realized that Gareth was right. Cecilia watched, dumbfounded, as Gareth took a Swiss army knife out of his pocket, opened a small blade, and inserted it between the floorboards, prying one of them up without much effort. Gareth stared into the hole for a second, then sat back heavily on the floor, shaking his head.

"What's in there?" Cecilia asked breathlessly, her face bright with anticipation.

Gareth reached in and pulled out a small tin box. The lid was slightly warped as if it had been opened and closed numerous times. He gripped the edges and the lid popped off easily. I leaned over to examine the contents and gasped. Inside was a tangle of women's jewelry and, sitting right on top, I could make out a small golden butterfly. I plucked it out with my fingers and as it came, the chain caught on something—a name badge that read 'Kelli'. Kelli with an i. I showed both of them to Gareth and Cecilia wordlessly.

"I never thought I'd see the day when two cold cases got solved at the same time," Cecilia said quietly.

"Maybe more than two," I answered, rummaging around in the box. "There are at least six other pieces of jewelry in here, including a pearl choker that looks like it might be from the 1920s. And this," I held up a delicate gold ring with a black onyx and diamonds in the setting, "is very distinctive."

Cecilia exhaled slowly and sat down on the displaced couch. "I'm going to have my work cut out for me, not only finding out who these victims might be, but trying to explain how we discovered the evidence in the first place."

"It won't be hard," Gareth started. "We've come up with some pretty rational explanations over the years—" Without warning, the ground began to rumble and the cabin started to shake. Cecilia remained seated, oblivious to the noise and tremors.

"What is it?" he shouted.

"Something's coming!" I answered. "I can feel it!"

Cecilia stared at us in amazement. "What are you talking about? And why are you both yelling?"

"Cecilia, I need you to trust us right now. There's something happening and it might be dangerous. Please, go into the bathroom and shut the door until we tell you to come out," I ordered her. She pulled back her jacket and pointed to her sidearm. "Believe me, that won't help," I said sternly.

She looked wildly between Gareth and me. He gestured with his chin towards the bathroom decisively. "Go in and lock the door behind you. Stay in there until it's safe."

She had no choice but to do as we asked. She'd no sooner shut the door behind her and we heard the click of the lock when it felt like all the air had just been sucked out of the room. Gareth and I had no idea what to prepare for—had Berith regained his strength and found us? In the vacuum of silence that followed, I held my breath again, this time in fear. Then the silence was broken by a deep, angry sob and a figure appeared before us. Samuel Bell had come home.

17

SAMUEL: REPRISE

He was dressed in a hospital gown and wore nothing on his feet. He was thinner than I remembered, his cheeks sunken and deep scars around his eyes where he'd clawed at them, trying to gouge them out. He stared at us in confusion. "Who are you? And what are you doing here in my house?"

I was inexplicably furious. "Who am *I*? I'm the sister of the last little girl you murdered, you bastard! Gareth, it's Samuel Bell. Get the bag—we have a malevolent to destroy!"

Gareth went for the door, but Samuel put his hands up. "Wait!" he implored. "Please, give me a chance to explain!"

"Explain what?" I demanded. "How you stole her and strangled her to satisfy some kind of bloodlust? If you weren't already dead, I'd kill you myself!"

"I had no choice! It wasn't me—it was Berith. He made me do all of those terrible things. I tried to fight him but I was powerless. I would never have hurt your sister or the rest of those children otherwise—and now I'm back to stop him from hurting anyone else. No more playing servant to his master."

Gareth paused and looked to me for direction. I was torn. How could I believe what Bell was telling me, that he really was as much an innocent victim as the children he'd killed—and women, potentially? On the other hand, if Bell was lying, why was he here? Why hadn't he immediately gone to Berith's aid, or if he couldn't do that, why hadn't he attacked us himself? I stared at him, a pathetic figure, hunched, shivering and terrified, and decided to give him the benefit of the doubt. "All right," I said finally. "You have one chance—start talking."

"Berith took me when I was 27 years old. He appeared to me in the form of my father, Abel, who'd abandoned me as a baby and left me with an abusive mother. I was in foster care for years, then lived alone in peace until right before my birthday, when *he* showed up, claiming that he wanted to make amends, take me here to the family cabin. I was no sooner in his car when he jumped me and knocked me out. That's the last thing I remember—everything else is like something from a nightmare that I couldn't wake up from and I was never sure what was real. The only time in the last decade that I was even remotely conscious was right after I crashed the car into that tree out there. I woke up for a minute, then the monster who'd controlled me for so many years fled, leaving me an empty shell until I was able to finally die."

"And how exactly did you accomplish that?" I asked skeptically, not even trying to keep the anger from my voice. "Rumour has it you caused your own death, but how do we know Berith didn't have something to do with it? Maybe he was fed up with your inability to help him in a vegetative state so he freed you to do his bidding from beyond the veil."

Gareth stood by the door, waiting for the signal to get his equipment. He could easily dispatch something like

Samuel Bell, and I couldn't wait for even a hint that Bell was still in league with The Seventh Devil.

"No," Samuel Bell answered. "I've been fighting him ever since the accident. It's taken everything I have to keep him at bay while I lay there, tortured by the knowledge of what he'd forced my body to do. It was a living hell, and I thought I'd go mad, until yesterday, when I heard a different voice. It was far away at first, but then it came closer and closer until I could make out what it was saying. 'You're a special boy, Samuel Chambers. Remember—you're smarter than you think and stronger than you know.'"

"Why would you believe it wasn't just Berith, up to his usual tricks?"

"Because the last time I heard that voice, I was ten years old. And I hadn't thought of it since. It was my grade 5 teacher, Ms. Ward. She was the one who reported my mother's abuse and it was the last thing she said to me before I was put into foster care. I had to switch schools and I never saw her again. I'd forgotten about her until I heard her out there in the black. And it gave me the strength I needed to finally escape."

"So you somehow killed yourself?" I asked.

"I reached out to the voice, and the spirit of my teacher appeared, older than she was when I knew her, but still with the kindest face. She took my hand and led me into the void where I became separate from myself. I could see my own body lying there, trapped and useless, and I did to myself what these hands had done to so many—I wrapped them around my own throat and began to squeeze. *He* came, thundering and furious, but Ms. Ward wouldn't let him stop me—she fought him the way I wished that I could have. I kept throttling the body, all that remained of Samuel Bell, until there was no life left. And as it died, I floated away. She faded, her hand still stretched out to me, and then she was gone. Ms. Ward had saved me for the second time."

"Okay," I said, still inwardly seething. I relayed a quick summary to Gareth, wishing that Mort's gift to him of seeing spirits hadn't been a one-time only deal. "Say we buy your story. What now? What's the plan?"

Samuel was about to speak when there was a sudden sharp knock at the door. Gareth, who was standing right next to it, jumped in surprise. "'What now?' is right!" he exclaimed. He peered out the window onto the porch and sighed. "You'll never guess who's here." Then the doorknob started rattling and I didn't need to guess.

"You better get it," I said. "Remember what happened to me last time?"

Gareth pulled the door open and The Portend was standing there on the porch. He was wearing the same eccentric Victorian style garb with a velvet jacket and pants and ruffled lace collar, and he still had the same sinister grin on his face. Mort Sterven, the epitome of good taste with his expensive bespoke suit, Italian leather shoes, and fine wristwatch, was at the bottom of the steps, squinting up through his mirrored sunglasses at the clear blue sky with distaste. "Honestly. This dimension is so bright—I don't know how you stand it," he said, turning to face the door and mounting the stairs. The Portend moved aside silently to allow Mort to enter the cabin.

"I see you got the party invitation," Gareth said sarcastically. "And you brought a friend."

Mort laughed. "Very clever. Yes, sorry to gatecrash, but we have a pick-up to make." He looked at his wristwatch, then back at Samuel Bell. "Time's a-ticking. I don't know how you managed to evade The Portend and end up here, but we have a very different destination in mind for you."

Samuel Bell started backing away, horrified. "No! You don't understand! Berith is coming for Thomas and I need to save him—I can't let my son become a Vessel for that monster!"

Mort hesitated, then turned to The Portend. "Interesting. What are your thoughts?"

The Portend considered for a moment, then he grinned, sightless behind his black lunettes, and whispered, "*Not yet.*"

Gareth had come over to stand next to me. "What's going on?" he asked, sotto voce, but Mort heard him.

"Has it worn off already? Honestly, you humans are such an imperceptive bunch. Here." He waved his hand disdainfully at Gareth, in the same motion that he'd used at Mitchell's house in Halifax, and immediately, Gareth gasped. "Better?" Mort asked. Gareth nodded, speechless. "Carrying on," Mort continued, addressing Samuel Bell. "The Portend is in agreement. What did you have in mind?"

I leaned over and whispered to Gareth, "I take it you can see Bell now?"

"Yeah." He gestured. "He looks terrible."

"As he should," I answered. "He says he knows Berith is coming after Thomas and he wants to help stop him."

Samuel continued. "I know where my son is, but Berith will use me to get to him. I need your help to get him away, take him somewhere safe. The woman, his mother, can't safeguard him. In fact, that's why Berith chose her. He has a certain type—he doesn't want the Vessels to grow up happy. Misery and abuse make them more vulnerable, easier to turn when the time comes, and Thomas is no exception. But he's just a child! He deserves more than a life of horror."

Mort considered for a moment. "Where's the child?"

"In Thunder Bay," I interjected.

Samuel looked at me, shocked. "How did you know that?"

"My sister—the one you *killed*—told me. She's concerned about him too. Even after everything you did to her, she still wants to protect Thomas." I didn't care if I sounded bitter—I *was* bitter. It seemed so unfair to me that Samuel Bell's son was alive and well, while Harmony was in the ground, her bones all that was left of her. But I wasn't spiteful enough to refuse Bell's request—there was more at stake than Thomas's safety. If Berith got to him first, he would gain the strength he needed to stay in this dimension and kill who knows how many more innocents.

Samuel took in what I said without flinching and responded, not in anger or defensiveness but with what seemed like genuine remorse. "I can't bring your sister back. Believe me, the knowledge that I was responsible for her death is horrifying to me. All I ever wanted was to live a quiet life, and I can't even have that in death. Please—will you help me?"

I sighed. "Harmony said Thomas was within sight of the Sleeping Giant. It's a large monument, so it's going to be difficult to find him. Believe me, we're working on it."

"The monument? No, that's not what she meant. It's the name of his school, Sleeping Giant Public School. He lives nearby. And if I know that, then so does Berith, so you need to hurry. He's getting stronger and soon no one will be able to stop him."

"We were on our way to Thunder Bay as soon as we were done here. The faster you answer our questions, the quicker we'll be on our way," Gareth said.

"Anything."

"First, why are there trophies hidden under the floor? Who do they belong to?" Gareth held up the golden butterfly. "We know this pendant was taken from Anna Lewis, but what about the others?"

Samuel sighed. "It's what he makes us do. When the time comes, the current Vessel must find a surrogate, someone who will bear the next Vessel before the current one wears out. The human form isn't strong enough to be inhabited for more than fifty years—Berith is a hard taskmaster. Most of those—trophies, you called them—are taken as a prize, or a record of progenity. But sometimes, when the Vessel is incompetent, or the woman is reluctant, the item is removed by force, to cover up the crime. My… father, Abel—he was sensitive. In another life, he would have been an artist. And though Berith corrupted him, it went against his nature to do what Berith required of him. So the monster took over."

"Thank you," Gareth said, then turned to me. "I think we can safely say that Abel Bell killed Anna Lewis. We can finally give her family the answers they were looking for."

"But that doesn't solve the problem of what to do with this one," Mort interjected.

None of us knew what to say. Then The Portend pounded his cane into the floor. "Right," Mort said, sighing. He examined his fingernails and then picked an imaginary piece of lint off his suit.

"Right *what*?" I asked.

"The Portend will take him to…the holding area. You and Gareth can toddle along to 'Thunder Bay' and find the child."

"Wait!" Samuel exclaimed. "Do I…do I have to wear this for the rest of eternity?" He gestured at the hospital gown. It was open at the back and very short.

I couldn't help but stifle a laugh. "You can wear whatever you want. Most spirits are content with the clothes they died in, but I see your point. You can choose something different if you'd like."

Samuel closed his eyes and concentrated for a minute. Suddenly, he seemed to wink out and then back into our sphere, only now, he was wearing work pants, a t-shirt, and a jacket with a logo on it. "These clothes," he said. "It was the only point in my life when I was truly happy, that I felt like I was someone instead of no one."

For the first time, I realized that his eyes were the brightest blue I'd ever seen, and as much as I wanted to hate him, the look on his face, so wistful and full of sorrow, made me feel a twinge of empathy. I quickly tried to shove it away but it lingered. "You'll save Thomas, won't you?" he asked, his trust fully with us.

"I promise," I said. With that, The Portend pounded his cane on the floor once more and he and Samuel disappeared.

18

THE SLEEPING GIANT

Once The Portend and Samuel were gone, we were all silent for a while. Gareth leaned against the counter, lost in thought. Mort pulled out a chair and sat at the small kitchen table, staring impassively at the room through his reflective lenses. My mind was racing with what Samuel had told us, and I was about to suggest calling Wes and letting him know that we'd narrowed down the search for Thomas when the bathroom door suddenly creaked open. I started, completely forgetting its lone occupant had been in there for over half an hour.

Cecilia poked her head out and looked around, catching my eye. "Sorry," she whispered. "But it's been so quiet—I thought maybe it was okay to come out now." I nodded and she stepped tentatively into the room. Then she saw Mort. "Who the hell are you?" she demanded. "This is a crime scene—you shouldn't be here."

Mort smiled his most charming smile. "I'm a friend of the family."

Cecilia narrowed her eyes. "Do I know you? You look familiar."

Mort rose to his feet and smoothed out the creases in his suit. "I believe we crossed paths when you were younger. I was visiting your grandmother, if I'm not mistaken. I'm surprised you remember—most people don't. However," he addressed Gareth. "I really must be off. So much to do, so little time and all of that. I'll catch up with you once you have the boy." He opened the cabin door, stepped through, and vanished.

Cecilia blinked hard. "Did he just...disappear? Who was he? And how on earth could he have known my grandmother? She died when I was four—wait! I thought it was a nightmare, something triggered by her death, but he *was* there! A man came to the door. I answered it because everyone else was at her bedside. He wasn't wearing a suit or sunglasses, just a weird long robe, but it was definitely him! My god—is he...?"

"Death, yes," I answered. She staggered to one side and Gareth rushed over to support her, leading her to the couch. "It's all right. He wasn't here to take anyone. He's helping us with our case."

She leaned forward, her head in her hands and said faintly, "Case? The one you were talking about with Samuel Bell while I was in the bathroom? I couldn't hear him, of course, just your side of the conversation, but I'm assuming it was really him, based on all the other bizarre things that have happened since yesterday."

"Uh...," I didn't know how to respond. Although she had a mind that was more open than most people, I wasn't sure how much information would be too much for her to handle. Gareth stepped in.

"Abel Bell killed Anna Lewis. I'm sure her parents will be able to identify the pendant, especially since it's inscribed on the back, so that's one case solved, as well as the Kelli Needham disappearance. The rest of the objects in that box belong to other women whose lives were cut short by either Abel Bell or maybe even his father or grandfather.

You've got a lot of work ahead of you, and we're sorry to leave you to it, but we need to go."

"But how do I explain this to my superiors? Are they seriously going to believe that I just came here on a random whim and found evidence of serial killings? Ugh." She sagged back into the couch cushions, a worried expression on her face.

"Why not?" Gareth shrugged. "Why not tell them that while you were examining the burial site, you learned that Samuel Bell had died? It triggered a memory about the rumours of Samuel following in his father's footsteps. You also remembered the Tia Dawson case and how the killer had kept trophies so, on a hunch, you came here and searched until you found the evidence you needed. You can leave Gareth and me out of it completely."

Cecilia brightened and sat up. "That just might work. Why would anyone doubt me? It's a much more plausible story than the truth."

"All right," Gareth said briskly. "Contact us if you need us; otherwise, we'll be in touch soon. Come on, Verity."

We left Cecilia sitting on the couch in the cabin lost in thought, staring at the contents of the tin box. Once we got settled into the truck, I looked up routes to Thunder Bay. "It's quicker if we take the ferry, but we've missed the last sailing. What do you want to do? Wait until tomorrow morning or start driving now? It's just about 18 hours from here—we could probably make it to Sudbury by tonight, and then leave first thing in the morning, get to Thunder Bay by dinner."

"Or we could take shifts, drive through the night and be there tomorrow morning. I know, I know," he said sympathetically, "you hate driving at night. But I don't think we have any time to waste. Remember what Samuel said. Who knows when Berith might be powerful enough to stop us?"

"Agreed. I just wish we could go home first," I answered sadly. After everything that had happened recently, I was missing Horace and Quentin more than I thought I would. Over the last year, we'd really become a family; their warmth and kindness had sustained me when I was going through difficult times, and our visit from Samuel Bell certainly counted as one of the worst in recent memory. At least I could call Wes, hear the sound of his reassuring voice. He answered right away, and when I told him what we'd learned, he was excited.

"With that kind of information, I can find Thomas pretty quickly. Give me around an hour."

"Do I want to know how you'll track him down?" I asked, laughing.

"The less said the better," he answered, laughing along with me. "Talk soon."

We'd just gone through Wiarton and I was wishing we'd had time to stop and take pictures with the giant groundhog at the Wiarton Willie memorial when my phone rang. "That was fast. Tell me you have good news," I said eagerly.

"Thomas Blackstone. Grade 5 student in Mr. Murrell's class at Sleeping Giant Public School. Home address: 45 Greenpark Street. Mother's name: Madeline Blackstone. How's that for speed?"

"You're amazing," I said.

"Oh, I don't know about that. Fantastic, maybe. But hey, you're not so bad yourself, so, um, maybe when you get back, we can discuss our mutual awesomeness further…."

I suddenly felt shy—I'd never had anyone flirt with me before, if that's what he was intending, and I stammered, "Of course, sure, see you soon," then quickly hung up.

Gareth looked at me out of the corner of his eye. "Got what we need?"

I nodded, hoping that my face hadn't gone red. I relayed Wes's information to Gareth and then settled back, trying to rest before my driving shift started. It was hard—

my thoughts were in turmoil and I was struggling with a terrible internal conflict after finding myself empathizing with Samuel Bell back at the cabin. Bell was the physical manifestation of the evil that had killed my sister, and having anything other than abject hatred for him felt like I was betraying Harmony. Still, when I saw him in my mind's eye, first as a small boy taken away from an abusive mother, spending his childhood and teen years in foster care, then as a young man proudly wearing a factory uniform and knowing that was the only time in his life that he was happy, I couldn't help but feel incredibly sorry for him.

I sat for a while, watching the scenery roll by and holding back tears. Gareth had the radio on low, and the murmuring voices and the hum of the road lulled me until I finally dozed off. I began to dream, and in that dream, Harmony came to me. "Don't be angry at Samuel, Veevee. All he wanted was to get away." She was surrounded by fog. She looked behind her and reached out her hand. Samuel Bell stepped out of the cloudy mist, and I felt a scream building in my throat as he took her hand in his own and held it. Right before the scream let loose, the truck jerked and the motion woke me up.

"Damn stop-and-go traffic!" Gareth snarled. He heard me breathing raggedly. "Hey, you okay? Don't worry—I'm not tailgating."

"I know." I yawned and stretched, hoping that the motion disguised my distress. "Is it almost time for my shift? I don't mind starting early."

Gareth and I chatted for a while until he got sleepy and climbed into the back seat of the truck, making me promise to let him take over at 3 am. But I stayed behind the wheel, hoping that focusing on the road would take my mind off the dream, stopping only for gas, even after my shift was finished. The last thing I wanted was to fall asleep again. I drove until dawn; Gareth didn't stir until the sun's rays glinted through the windshield and he sat up groggily.

"Where are we?" he groaned, trying to unbend his stiff knees. "Hey, is that the Terry Fox monument?! Why didn't you wake me up?"

I shrugged. "You looked so peaceful. And I wasn't tired. We're almost there, so you can take over now if you want." I found a parking lot and turned in. Gareth unfolded himself out of the back seat gingerly and straightened his back.

"Oof," he said. "Nothing like lying in one position for hours. But I was really out—I don't remember a thing after Wawa."

I envied him—I wished I could forget the past few hours, visions of Harmony with Samuel Bell haunting my mind. I shook it off and said, "I put the address in the GPS. It's not far from here and it's still early. Do you want to get breakfast first?"

Gareth nodded and blinked hard, trying to energize himself. The parking lot I'd pulled into had a small all-night diner attached to a gas station, so we fueled up the truck first, then ourselves. After polishing off a literal mound of bacon and toast, we were both ready to carry on.

Greenpark Street was quiet so early in the morning and few of the houses had any lights on yet. We stopped in front of number 45, the brakes on the truck squealing slightly and disrupting the silence. The small post-war bungalow was identical to the house in my dream where I'd first seen Thomas, an ordinary house with nothing that set it apart from its neighbours. Gareth put down the windows, filling the cab of the truck with cool, sweet air and we waited for a moment, watching for any sign of life. "Do you think we should—" I started to say, when a small cry came from inside the house, a sound of despair and fear. I jumped out of the truck's passenger side, Gareth following close behind. We ran up the driveway to the side entrance and I peered in through the sidelight. I could see a woman lying on the floor of the kitchen, and a young boy was on his knees, crawling around her, shaking her. I tried the knob—the door was locked, but at the sound of it rattling, the boy looked up, terrified.

"Thomas?" I called out. "What's happening? Let us in!"

The boy ran to the door and flung it open. He was slight, with ash-blonde hair, and looked exactly as he had in my dream. He was wearing pajamas, and where the sleeve had ridden up, there was a bruise on his wrist. "I know you!" he exclaimed. "You're the girl from my dreams! Help me!"

He hurried back to the unconscious woman on the floor and sank down next to her, trying to revive her. "My mother!" he cried. "She's done it again!"

"Done what?" Gareth asked. He knelt down next to the woman and felt her pulse. "She's alive," he whispered to me. "But barely."

The woman on the floor was desperately thin, with hollowed out cheeks and stringy hair. Her mouth hung open, exposing teeth that were broken and blackened, and her bare arms were covered with sores. The boy gestured to the kitchen counter where a pipe lay in an ashtray. "She was supposed to get groceries yesterday but she came home with that instead. I don't know what to do!"

"Call 911," I said to Gareth, but as he was dialing, the woman stirred.

"Thomas," she murmured. "You have to save Thomas. I can't protect him. Please, take him away from here before he comes."

"Who's coming?" I asked.

Her eyes opened wide with horror. "He is the Seventh but not the least. He is older than time and the eater of souls. He is the Seventh but not the least! HE IS THE SEVENTH BUT NOT THE LEAST!! HE IS COMING!!" She screamed then fell back, unconscious. Thomas started to cry.

"It's all right," I said. I reached out to him but he flinched and scuttled backwards across the kitchen tiles. My heart broke, but I was firm. "My friend is calling for an ambulance, but we have to leave. Your mother wants us to protect you. Will you come with us?" Thomas hesitated then nodded, wiping the tears from his cheeks. "Okay. Quickly now, go to your room and gather up some things. We need to leave as soon as possible."

Thomas ran from the kitchen. Gareth looked at me questioningly. "What else can we do?" I asked. He nodded in silent assent. There were faint sirens in the distance, coming closer. Thomas skidded back into the room with a small knapsack stuffed with clothes. A worn teddy bear stuck out of the top, its eyes winking in the weak morning sunlight, and again, my heart clenched. "This way," I told him, pointing to the truck. We hurried out to the sidewalk before any of the neighbours heard the sirens and peeked out of their windows in curiosity. Gareth slid behind the wheel, put the truck in gear, and we sped away.

19

THE ECHO

We drove for two hours without stopping, Gareth gripping the steering wheel tightly and me looking behind us in the side view mirror, vigilant, worried that someone had seen us outside the Blackstone house and tipped off the police. Thomas was huddled fearfully in the corner of the back seat, his arms wrapped tight around his knapsack. He'd said nothing since we'd left the house; I wasn't sure if he was worried about his mother, or scared of us—either way, he looked miserable. Finally, it seemed as if we were in the clear, and I gestured to Gareth to pull over into a rest stop that overlooked rocky forest and a lake in the distance. He got out of the truck to give me a chance to talk to Thomas alone. I was glad; Gareth wasn't used to children and I doubted that either of them would be comfortable with each other at first. Once he was out of earshot, I swivelled in my seat.

"How are you?" I asked Thomas. He didn't reply; his eyes shifted away from me to the view from the window. Beneath his eyes there were dark circles like bruises. They matched the ones on his arm. "How did you get those?" I pointed. He pulled his arm back and hid it behind his knapsack. "It's okay. You can tell me. Was it your mother?"

"She gets mad," he whispered. "Mostly after she's been drinking with one of her boyfriends or...." He left the rest unsaid, both of us picturing the unmoving body of Madeline Blackstone on the kitchen floor.

"You're safe here with us. My name is Verity, and that's Gareth." I pointed through the windshield at Gareth, who was standing with his back to us, contemplating the view, hands in his pockets.

"Is he—is he your dad?" Thomas asked.

I laughed lightly. "No, we just work together. But he's one of the good guys. You don't need to worry about him." I could see Thomas visibly relax, and inwardly shuddered to think about what his experience with his mother's 'boyfriends' had been like. "We're going to take you somewhere safe—you can trust us."

"I know," Thomas said. "That's what the girl told me, and I believe her."

"What girl?"

"The little girl in my dreams. She has long blonde hair and her name is—"

"Harmony," I finished for him. My sweet sister—even in the afterlife, she made people feel safe and cared for. "Do you dream about her a lot?"

"Sometimes. Especially when the man with the yellow eyes comes. She tries to keep him away from me but she can't hold him off anymore. I'm afraid to go to sleep. But I remember dreaming about you too—you were standing at the end of my driveway, watching me. How did you know where to find me?"

"That's a long story," I said. "But right now, we need to get going. We have other friends waiting for us, and they're all anxious to meet you." I gave the horn a light tap and Gareth looked over his shoulder towards us. I waved to him and he got back in the driver's seat.

"Plan?" he asked.

"Drive until dark, find somewhere to sleep for the night, then on to The Echo as fast as we can. Thomas, this is

Gareth. Gareth, Thomas." Gareth reached over the seat and held out his hand. Thomas took it and they shook solemnly. "Thomas wondered if you were my dad," I said with a mischievous glint in my eye. "But I told him we were just work partners."

Gareth cleared his throat and smiled tightly. "That's right." He turned the key in the ignition and revved the engine. "Everyone ready?"

We drove most of the day in silence, each of us lost in our own thoughts, stopping only for a quick picnic lunch at another rest stop, after which, I took a driving shift. Thomas stayed curled up in his corner of the back seat, and every now and then, our eyes made contact through the rear view mirror. He looked exhausted but refused to sleep, shaking himself awake whenever the urge to doze off started to overtake him, Finally, the sun went down, and I was desperate to swap my increasingly uncomfortable truck seat for a bed; the problem was, there were no campsites anywhere near us where we could hook up to electricity and water. "Can we splurge on a motel for tonight?" I asked Gareth. "I know we could just pull into a rest stop and sleep there in the trailer, but I haven't had a shower for two days."

"Agreed," Gareth said. "I need to charge the laptop anyway. Where's the nearest town?"

It was close to 9 p.m. when we pulled into the parking lot of the Come On Inn. "Cute," Gareth snorted.

"It's cheap," I countered. "And we need two rooms. I'll take Thomas and you can have a room all to yourself. We can do takeout for dinner—Thomas, you pick."

The boy's eyes lit up. "Could we get McDonald's?"

"McDonald's?" Gareth asked. "Seriously?"

Thomas's face fell. "I've never had McDonald's. My mother doesn't like to waste money on fast food. She says it's bad for your health."

Gareth snorted, and was about to say something, no doubt critical of Madeline Blackstone's hypocrisy, but

I interjected. "Of *course* we can get McDonald's. Burgers, fries, and shakes for everyone!"

Later, in Gareth's room, we ate at a small table. Thomas dug in with gusto, his face beaming. "It's delicious!" he proclaimed through a mouthful of French fries. It was the first time that I'd seen him smile.

Gareth looked up from his phone and stared at his quarter-pounder in dismay. "Well, it's *something*."

After dinner, I needed to speak to Gareth privately. "Thomas, can you grab your knapsack and go next door to get ready for bed? I'll be there in a minute, okay?" He nodded, still slurping on his milkshake, and left the room. I sat down on the edge of the bed heavily. "Any word about Thomas's mother?"

Gareth held up his phone. "I've been scanning the local news sites, but nothing. I assume they took her to the hospital—if she died from the overdose there, who knows when it would be reported publicly?"

"Maybe we should call. See if she's a patient there—or not. I won't give them my name."

He thought for a minute, then shook his head. "As much as I'd like to know too, if you call, they'll have your number. And if they have your number, they'll have no trouble finding out your name. I really think it's better to wait until we get back to The Echo."

"Or I could call Wes, see if he can look into it. Plus, what if people think that Thomas has been abducted?"

"Verity, leave it for now. Thomas hasn't asked about his mother, and what if we find out that she really has died? What do we tell him then? No, it's safer to do all of this from home base. Once we get there, we can call, let the authorities know where Thomas is, and that we had permission to take him with us. Okay?"

I sighed. As much as I really wanted to know if Madeline had survived, it wouldn't do any good if we got pulled over and hauled back to Thunder Bay on kidnapping charges. I said goodnight and went to my room. Thomas was already in his pajamas and watching cartoons. I had a quick shower, then got ready for bed myself. When I came out of the bathroom, he was still sitting in the room's lone chair, fixed to the television.

"All right, buddy. It's really late. Time to put the lights out."

Reluctantly but without argument, he turned off the TV and slid into the twin bed closest to the door. I climbed into the other bed and sighed with relief as my body sank into the thick mattress. I lay there for a minute, luxuriating, then Thomas broke the silence. "Is…is my mother going to be okay?"

I turned onto my side and propped myself up on one elbow. In the dim light, I couldn't help noticing how much he looked like Samuel. Thomas's hair was lighter, but they both had the same haunted eyes. "I don't know," I told him honestly. "We hope so, right?"

"Hmm," he muttered. I wasn't sure if he was agreeing with me or not, and after what I'd seen of the bruises on his arms and the drug paraphernalia in the house, I couldn't blame him if he wasn't.

"What's 'The Echo'?" he asked.

"The Echo? That's where Gareth and I work. We live there too when we're not on the road, with our friends Horace and Quentin." I laughed at the way his eyes widened. "It's a big house. Lots of rooms for everybody. Including you. You can stay there with us until…well, as long as you need to. At least until your mother is all better. Come on now—you really need to get some sleep."

He turned over with his back to me, and it wasn't long before I could hear him breathing deeply. There were crickets outside, and as much as I wanted to keep lying there and thinking, their chirping lulled me until I was breathing deeply as well. I was right in the middle of a dream, a nice one for a change, where I was walking through a field of long grass. Water rushing over rocks murmured in the distance, and I was just about to dip my toes into a cool, clear stream when a loud shriek woke me with a start. Thomas was sitting straight up in bed, his eyes staring blankly ahead, his face pale with terror.

"Thomas! What's wrong?"

I threw off my covers and went over, shaking his shoulder gently. He continued to stare straight ahead as if he was in a trance. I shook him again but he still didn't respond. I was about to go next door and get Gareth when he whispered, "The gate. He wants me to go through the gate."

I paused, my hand on the doorknob. "What gate? Who wants you to go through the gate?"

"The man with the yellow eyes. He wants me to go through the gate, but I don't want to. I know if I do, I'll die and *I don't want to die!*" He started to cry hysterically. I ran back and sat next to him on the bed with my arm around him. He flinched slightly but then he leaned into me, sobbing. Finally, he calmed down and looked up at me with a tear-drenched face. "Can I have my teddy bear? I know I'm not supposed to, that it's a baby toy, but I really need it."

"Of course," I said, reaching over to grab his knapsack. I pulled the bear out and handed it to him.

He clutched it tight to his chest and whispered, "You won't tell my mom, will you?"

I hugged him, imagining what kind of mother would deprive her child of comfort. "What's his name?" I asked.

"*Her*," he corrected me. "Her name is Melody."

I blanched. Another ghost from the past making an appearance—Melody Benoit, one of The Swamp Killer's victims. Was it just a coincidence or had she somehow made a connection with Thomas as well? "There's nothing wrong with having a special friend. Your secret is safe with me," I said. He nestled down under the blankets, the teddy tucked under one arm. "I'm here if you need anything, Thomas."

I didn't remember closing my eyes, but after what seemed like a moment later, the crickets had changed to birdsong and the morning sun was streaming in through the window. I woke up Thomas and barely had time to brush my teeth and get dressed before Gareth knocked on the door.

"There's a continental buffet in the motel office," he said. "Let's grab something for the road and be on our way."

It was almost five hours from Sudbury to home, just in time for lunch. I called The Echo main line to tell Horace to expect us but there was no answer, so I left a message on the machine. Next, I called Wes. He didn't pick up either. I tried again an hour later. And then another hour later. Still no answer from anyone. "Weird," I said to Gareth quietly. "I wonder where they all are."

"Probably out shopping. Or maybe outside, doing some work on the house."

I laughed. "Horace? Outside work? Shopping is way more likely." Still, I was slightly unnerved by the lack of response—surely Horace would have checked his voicemail and responded by now.

Then, as we were finally driving down the back road towards home, my misgivings were confirmed. "Look!" I exclaimed to Gareth, pointing upwards. Right above the area where The Echo was located, there was a strange yellow glow in the sky. As we got closer, the glow seemed to intensify and appeared translucent, cascading from the sky down to the ground, creating a ring of shimmering, roiling fog that obscured the house and property. We stopped at the head of the laneway, not sure how to proceed—the sickly yellow light and murky fog were creating some kind of barrier and I didn't know what crossing through it might do to us.

Gareth got out of the truck and stood watching, one hand on the truck's hood, the other shielding his eyes from the light's eerie brilliance. I got out of the passenger side and stood next to him. "What the hell *is* that?" he asked.

An ominous voice from behind us answered. "It's Berith. He's here."

We both whirled around. Mort and The Portend had joined us.

20

THE GATE

"Berith?!" I exclaimed. "How is that even possible? You said he was still too weak to attack us!"

Mort took off his mirrored sunglasses. It was the first time I'd seen him without them. His eyes were a pale, icy gray framed by long dark lashes and right now, there were worry lines creasing his cheeks on either side of them. He frowned and squinted at the sky. "Apparently, I made an unfortunate miscalculation. I assumed, incorrectly, that Berith had fled to the other side of the gate, his tail between his legs. Instead, we've learned that he was biding his time, absorbing the energy of other, lesser malevolents until his power had been temporarily restored."

As I stood there, incredulous, a tendril of fog snaked its way towards us. "Stand back," Mort ordered. We all hurried to the other side of the road, away from the encroaching mist. "Don't let it touch you." I pulled Thomas behind me. "I wouldn't worry about the boy," Mort said. "Berith needs him too much to harm him. Still, that vapour can be very unpleasant if you come into contact with it."

"Then how do we get to the house?" I exclaimed. "What about Horace and Quentin? And Wes? They must be in there—in the fog—how can we save them?" I was beside myself, thinking of them in The Echo, maybe overcome by Berith or worse.

The Portend thumped his cane hard into the ground, causing Mort to nod and put his mirrored aviators back on. "The Portend is correct as always. Stand back."

"Stand back? What are you going to do?"

Mort smiled enigmatically. "I have a gate of my own to open." He made a gesture and The Portend removed his top hat, placing it carefully in the middle of the road. Mort snapped his fingers three times in succession and the top hat began to vibrate. The vibrations became more intense and then suddenly, a white light shot out of the hat, travelling around the ring of dark fog. As we watched, luminous figures appeared within the light, taking form and shape, assuming positions along the perimeter. I gasped in recognition as Melody Benoit stepped away from The Portend's hat, and I was about to nudge Gareth when I realized that many of the ghostly figures were people we knew—Nicky was there, and Clarice too, taking her daughter Melody's hand, while Uncle Pat strode forward to his place in the circle, giving me a wink as he passed by. Gareth made a sound like a strangled sob and I realized that Julia had appeared, a yellow bow in her hair, and just behind her was Jenny, who had made Harmony the origami unicorn. Dozens and dozens of spirits came forward; some were familiar, like little Arjun and Lorena DeSantos and even Samantha, our jigsaw puzzle ghost, and some were strangers in old-fashioned dress, like the spirits we'd crossed over in Halifax. We watched, speechless, until someone we knew better than anyone appeared.

"Mitchell!" Gareth called out joyously. Mitchell smiled and came over to us. "What's happening?"

"We heard the call," he said simply. "And we came. But I can't stop to talk—there's work to be done. We *will* defeat him for once and for all!"

Just then, I felt a tug at my hand. I looked down, and there was Harmony, my beautiful Harmony, radiating with an internal light that shone brighter than all the rest. "Don't worry, Veevee," she said. "We're all here to help." She pointed, and Samuel Bell stepped into the circle too, assuming his place with the others. Finally, the parade of spirits ceased and they all took their spots along the edge of the fog, joining their ghostly hands and waiting for a signal.

"Now!" Mort commanded, and as one, they closed their eyes and concentrated. White light radiated out of each of them, gaining strength, as if all the goodness and kindness that they possessed was made manifest. And where their inner light touched the dark fog, the fog recoiled, receding towards the house until finally it seemed to be sucked into The Echo as if caught in a vacuum. Finally, it diminished into a fine mist and vanished. As it did, the spirits in the circle began to disappear as well, swirling into the light and becoming one with it. From a distance, Mitchell waved to us as his form started to fade. The Portend reached down and picked up his top hat.

"Mitchell, wait!" I called out, but he was gone. "So soon?" I asked The Portend.

He nodded, his eyes hidden behind those dark lenses, and as he placed the hat back onto his head, the circle of light dissipated, leaving only Harmony behind. "Why are you still here?" I whispered, hoping that no one would notice.

She laughed and the sound was joy to my ears. "Because *he's* still here. But I can help. Thomas needs to stay with me—I can keep him safe from that." She pointed towards the house and my heart lurched when I saw what she meant. My beloved Echo, the only real home I'd ever known, had become one of the bad houses—the door was a yawning jaw full of sharp, bloody teeth and the windows were dead eyes. Everything was silent and still.

"No!" I whispered. I started to move forward but Gareth put out his arm to stop me, watching Mort for some kind of direction. Thomas was standing on the gravel shoulder, uncertain of what was happening, but worried nevertheless. Harmony went to him and he stared at her in wonderment. She whispered something in his ear and he nodded, walking away with her down the road.

"I know you want to go rushing in, but we need to proceed with caution," Mort advised. "We haven't vanquished Berith yet; we've won the battle but not the war."

Mort took the lead as we advanced towards the house. As we walked past the weeping willow, the tire swing swayed back and forth with a sinister creak. At the same time, the front door slowly opened and Horace stepped out.

"Horace!" I cried, racing towards him. Then I stopped. He was stiff, staring at us in an unsettling way. "Horace?"

Then his eyes flashed yellow and he smiled, a gruesome grin that let me know without a doubt that it wasn't really Horace I was looking at. He pulled his pocket watch out of his waistcoat, glanced at it and sneered. "It's about time."

"Time for what?" Gareth called out from right behind me. His voice quavered; he was as unnerved as I was.

"Time to end this! Give me the boy!"

"Where are Quentin and Wes?" I demanded. "What have you done with them?"

"Oh," the fake Horace gestured broadly at an upper window. "They're patiently waiting for you to deliver to me what is mine. But if you don't…" He left the threat hanging in the air. I heard a faint sound and looked up. Wes and Quentin were banging on the window of one of the upper bedrooms, presumably locked inside. I could see Wes mouthing "Verity!" Suddenly, the glass shattered and Quentin yelled, "It's Berith! He's taken Horace! Free him!"

Horace waved his hand dismissively and the windowpane seemed to magically repair itself; Quentin's voice became muffled and incomprehensible. "Why don't we go inside?" Horace offered, "and discuss this like civilized… beings?" He turned on his heel and disappeared through the front door, leaving us no choice but to follow. The inside of the house was cold and still; the faint banging from upstairs was the only sound. We made our way into the kitchen where Berith, inhabiting Horace's body, sat waiting. At the sight of us, he snickered. "I see you've brought some friends," he scoffed.

The Portend slammed his cane onto the kitchen floor, but Mort placed his hand over The Portend's and said quietly, "Bide your time, my friend." Then he addressed Berith. "You can't have the boy. Surely, you know by now that I won't let you. You've overextended your reach." Berith snorted in disdain and Mort continued softly, "We have such a long history together. Do you remember the old days? The balance? It worked, didn't it? So why ruin a good thing now? Go back to your realm and take what is rightfully yours, no more and no less. You can't defeat me—you know that. And if you relent, you may even be forgiven for your transgressions."

At the word 'forgiven', Horace's face twisted as Berith became incensed. "Forgiven?! How dare you presume, you supercilious creature! *I* need forgiveness from *you*?! NEVER!!" He rose from his chair, and as he did, something incredible happened. Mort made a swirling gesture with his hand and suddenly, he began to transform. The bespoke cashmere suit, the Italian leather shoes, the exceptionally fine wristwatch, even the aviator sunglasses began to dissolve and metamorphosize. Mort himself seemed to grow and expand until finally, a giant stood before us, garbed in a long, flowing robe, its face obscured by a cowled hood. Horace leapt to his feet and turned to run, but the robe continued to expand and reach towards him, enveloping and trapping Berith and his new Vessel within its folds. Horace struggled fruitlessly as the robe continued to imprison him within its embrace. "How dare you?! You have no right!" he howled with fury, trying to break free. "*She* will hear of this, and you will be punished!"

"She punish ME?! *She* is the one who sent me!" Mort boomed back. "The balance must be restored!" As Horace's eyes grew wide with shock, Mort seized the opportunity to redouble his efforts until finally, there was a wrenching gasp and Horace fell to the floor of the kitchen, clutching his chest, still trapped in the embrace of the robe's unnaturally long sleeves.

"What's happening?" I shrieked, as Horace's face turned gray. I ran forward, Gareth on my heels, but The Portend extended his cane, stopping us in our tracks, and speaking for the first time.

"*Berith can only be defeated if the Vessel dies while he still inhabits it,*" The Portend whispered. "*Stay back.*"

We did as we were told, watching helplessly as Horace fought against the vice-like grip of the Reaper, becoming weaker, gasping for breath. I turned my face away and buried it in Gareth's chest. He wrapped his arms around me as I sobbed into his shirt. Finally, there was a last gasp and Horace succumbed to death, taking Berith with him. I broke away from Gareth, tears streaming down my face, and collapsed on the floor next to Horace, stroking his cheeks. Then, without warning, the kitchen door burst open. Wes came flying in, followed by Quentin who, at the sight of Horace, screamed, "No, it can't be!" Quentin fell onto his knees next to me, shoving me out of the way, and started CPR, his clenched fists compressing Horace's chest violently. I sat back on the kitchen tiles, barely registering that Wes had joined me on the floor, hands on my shoulders, watching, hoping against all hope that Quentin could perform a miracle. It seemed to go on for hours, Quentin alternating between chest compressions and artificial respiration while Mort, who had resumed his more familiar form, and The Portend watched impassively.

I couldn't take much more. "Do something!" I yelled at Mort, but he just shrugged.

"It will be what it is meant to be," he answered cryptically.

"Then help me!" Quentin implored, hanging his head in defeat. Suddenly he raised his head and stared up at The Portend. "You told me '*Not yet*.' Do you remember? What did you save me for if not for this?"

The Portend and Mort looked at each other. Mort tilted his head slightly and said, "It's been long enough." The Portend grinned. There was a sudden rush of air and then...Horace coughed. Quentin began to cry and kiss Horace's head in relief as he began to breath jaggedly.

"Thank you," Quentin sighed, caressing Horace's face.

Mort cleared his throat and The Portend nodded. They both turned and, right before they left the kitchen, Mort stopped. "I'm glad this all worked out for the best," he said. He pulled his mirrored sunglasses out of his suit pocket and put them on with a flourish.

"Wait!" I leapt to my feet. "You said 'she' sent you—who exactly is *she*?"

Mort smiled his most charming smile and The Portend grinned. "That's a story for another day," he said, then looked at his watch. "Time's a-ticking." He gestured to The Portend, who nodded once more, and without a sound, they both disappeared.

I laughed without even knowing why, and Wes kissed me on the cheek ecstatically. Horace's eyes flew open, and he looked around at us in amazement. "I found Mimi," he breathed. "My darling Mimi. I've brought her home."

♦ ♦ ♦

Much later, after Horace was safely tucked into his own bed, Quentin by his side in a wing chair watching him for any signs of a relapse, Gareth and I sat at the kitchen table with Thomas. I'd taken a moment, once we knew that Horace would recover and that Berith was finally gone, to call the hospital in Thunder Bay. Madeline Blackstone had survived the overdose, and after telling the nurse that I was her sister, I was put through to her room. I let her know that Thomas was fine. She paused for a moment, then told me that she was going into rehab, that she knew she couldn't be a proper mother to Thomas. She agreed that he could stay with us—for the time being at least—with the promise that she could come and visit him once she was clean. But she needed to know that Thomas understood her decision. We explained everything to him, and he listened solemnly.

"I'm okay staying here," he said. "Harmony told me that it was a good place. And maybe once my mother's better, she can come here too."

Just then, Wes entered the kitchen. Remembering that kiss earlier in the day, I lowered my eyes and hoped that Gareth couldn't see me blushing. Whether he could or not, he said to Thomas, "Uh, do you want to see the barn? It's got...hay." Despite the quirkiness of the invitation, Thomas's eyes lit up and he happily followed Gareth outside.

"So," Wes began.

"So," I repeated, trying not to smile.

"Any interest in discussing our mutual awesomeness now that everything seems to be back to normal?"

"Normal?" I laughed. "That'll be the day."

21

THOMAS

Thomas Blackstone looked out the window of his bedroom at The Echo. Aunt Veevee and Gareth had just pulled into the driveway, back from their visit with the parrot people. Thomas was excited; he wanted to know more about the swearing demon parrot that he'd heard everyone talking about. He ran downstairs and out the door, just in time to hear Gareth grumbling, "I still have feathers in my hair. Tell Horace no more animals!"

Thomas laughed. "Did you make the parrot better, Gareth?" he asked.

Gareth scowled and muttered something about 'that stupid bird' but Aunt Veevee smiled. "We did. And we'll tell you all about it at dinner. But right now, we have to get cleaned up." She pulled a feather out of her pocket and waved it mischievously under Thomas's nose, tickling him with it. "Why don't you stay out here and get some fresh air? You've been cooped up in your room all day reading, haven't you?"

Thomas smiled shyly. "Maybe a little."

Aunt Veevee and Gareth went into the house, and Thomas walked over to the weeping willow tree, flopping down on the grass next to the tire swing. "Mimi, what are you and Grace doing?" he asked.

The little girl on the tire swing threw her head back and giggled. "I'm trying to reach the moon!" she exclaimed, her body shimmering in the sunlight. Further up among the branches, an older girl sat, her translucent legs dangling in the air.

"Be careful you don't launch yourself too far, Mimi!" she cautioned.

Mimi planted her feet in the dirt, stopping the tire. She was staring at something over Thomas's shoulder. "Who's that?" she asked, curious but wary.

Thomas glanced back. There was a man standing there, an ordinary-looking man wearing work pants, a t-shirt and a jacket with a logo on it. His eyes were blue—the bluest that Thomas had ever seen. Thomas stood up and waved, and Samuel Chambers smiled and waved back. "Him?" Thomas said. "Don't worry about him. He's a friend."

EPILOGUE

THE OVERSEER

She paced the vast barren hallway, bristling with annoyance.

A small creature, gnarled, red, with eyes like hollows, gamboled towards her from out of the darkness.

"Well?" she demanded.

"It is done."

"And what was the outcome?" She was uncharacteristically nervous and tapped her foot against the black marble floor, the sound echoing high up in the vaulted ceiling.

"The Seventh is…no more."

She exhaled, realizing that she had been holding her breath. "And what of the Reaper?"

"On his way. With…" The creature paused and curled his lip in distaste. "…the grinning one."

"Thank you, Lutin," she responded. "You needn't be here when they arrive." She pulled a coin from within the folds of her cloak and held it out. The small creature plucked it from her fingers and examined it lovingly, turning it back and forth, watching it sparkle as it caught the weak light. He nodded and winked out of sight.

She waited, motionless, arms crossed over her chest, listening. In the distance, on the outer edges of the darkness, machinery hummed faintly. A fire burned somewhere and it crackled and popped while indistinguishable voices chittered softly. Then the air was sucked away and in the vacuum of silence that followed, footsteps approached.

She smiled. Without turning around, she spoke. "I heard that it went well."

Behind her, Mort Sterven gave The Portend a sidelong glance. The Portend grinned enigmatically and shrugged his shoulders. Mort cleared his throat. "A little *too* well. Overseer, we need to talk."

Also by Suzanne Craig-Whytock

The Seventh Devil

The Dome

Smile